Project
Soul

D.L. Ford

Psalm 32:8

DEDICATION

This book is dedicated to those who devote their lives to helping and protecting others. Sometimes all it takes is a kind word or a friendly smile to make someone's day. There are so many people out there who do that for a living every day, every week, every year. Thanks to all who give and sacrifice for others, and may you all be blessed.

Philippians 2:1-4 The Message (MSG)

If you've gotten anything at all out of following Christ, if his love has made any difference in your life, if being in a community of the Spirit means anything to you, if you have a heart, if you care— then do me a favor: Agree with each other, love each other, be deep-spirited friends. Don't push your way to the front; don't sweet-talk your way to the top. Put yourself aside, and help others get ahead. Don't be obsessed with getting your own advantage. Forget yourselves long enough to lend a helping hand.

CONTENTS

ACKNOWLEDGMENTS

1
A BORING EXISTENCE

The soft, crunching sound of paper bouncing off the wall was a reminder of just how bored Ted Crosby was. He wasn't quite sure which was worse, the fact he was shooting imaginary hoops with balled up pieces of paper yet again, or the fact he was so bored he actually knew the score and kept records of his accuracy. He decided the worst part was the knowledge this imaginary game always seemed to be the highlight of his day. The last five years of his life had been given to Pantheon Incorporated. Pantheon was one of the largest medical corporations in the country and the jobs they provided were a prime source of income and population for the small city of Tallinn. Although the pay was good, Ted never felt he had anything to show for it. Sure, he had a few expensive toys at home, and a decent bank account, but there always seemed to be something missing. It seemed like there was a void inside he could feel, yet not explain. When he left college, his dreams and goals were big. Do some advanced research, come up with miraculous cures, save the world, that kind of thing. Instead, he was trapped in a sea of corporate nonsense, politically correct rules and regulations, with the primary focus of everything being the profit margin and stock price. Every time he looked at the Five Year Service Award on his desk, his stomach knotted. All he ever wanted to do was make a difference, to make the world a better place. Instead, his bank account was full and his heart was empty. Those thoughts were suddenly disturbed by a soft nudge on the bottom of his chair.

"Time to wake up from your nap and think about work, Ted!"

Ted turned to see Christine, who occupied the office next to his, had entered his office without his knowing.

"I'm awake, I'm awake."

"Yeah, sure. Your mind was a million miles away in oblivion. Made it real easy to sneak in here."

"Okay, we'll have it your way. Why didn't you just let me rest in oblivion, in that case?"

Christine chuckled. "Because the big boss lady sent me here to come get you! Said something about having a special project for you."

"Wonderful. What kind of mood does she appear to be in today?"

"Oh, the usual."

"Great. Have the blood transfusions ready to go for me, would you?"

"You know it. Good luck, brave soldier!"

"Thanks. I'll probably need it."

Ted halfheartedly got up from his chair and headed slowly down the hallway towards the office of Olivia Wilson, the "boss lady," as they all called her behind her back, but only if they were feeling kind. The other names behind her back were far more derogatory. Everyone in the building thought of her as a cold, ruthless superior. Always more concerned about personal glory and profit than the well-being of any of the employees under her. Ted would rather be going to have a tooth pulled without anesthetics than to be facing her, but it was just one of the things he had to do to earn his paycheck. As he approached her office, he could see the office door partially open, a sign that she was waiting for him.

"Come right in, Mr. Crosby. Have a seat."

"And to what do I owe this honor, Ms. Wilson?"

"Close the door."

The tone of her voice gave him an icy feeling as he closed the door quietly behind himself. It was almost as if he had closed the passageway to the real world and was now trapped in her cold, calculating environment. It didn't help his impression one bit as he sat down in the leather chair across from her desk and sank deeply down into it, almost like sinking in quicksand. When he stopped sinking in the chair, his face was at a level much lower than hers causing him to look up at her. He had a feeling she had picked the chair just for that specific purpose.

"So what's up, boss?"

"I've checked your files. You're a smart guy, Crosby, probably overqualified for what we have you doing. I would guess you're pretty bored, too, aren't you?"

"Well…" He paused, knowing he should probably be careful about choosing his answer to the question. "I guess you could say that. I think I'm capable of more than what I've done lately."

"Precisely. How would you like a special assignment?"

"Special assignment?"

"Yes. Very special. Very confidential. You'd be reporting directly to me on this matter. No one else must know of it. Do you think you'd be interested?"

Every ounce of common sense within him was screaming to walk out the door, but the current state of his life was so boring, he was intrigued by the offer.

"So what does this secret mission entail, exactly?"

"Long before you were here, we employed an extremely intelligent scientist and physicist named Dr. Carter McCoy. He was very gifted in orthopedic surgery and neurosurgery as well."

"Oh, a real renaissance man, eh?"

"You don't know the half of it. He was a regular boy genius and always in a world of his own, learning as much as he could. We usually just stayed out of his way and let him do his research. Our company has made countless millions of dollars on the medicines and procedures he discovered by accident."

"By accident?"

"Yes, he had a grand theory he was working on he never shared with anyone. All his discoveries came while on the quest for the answers he sought. He made us so much money we never pushed for answers on that one. He's a bit of an eccentric person as well, so even in good times, it was hard to get through to him."

"That's a nice story, but how do I fit into it?"

"Seven years ago, he came down with a rare form of amyotrophic lateral sclerosis. As soon as he received the diagnosis, he left the company. We supported his decision and kept tabs on him."

"Isn't that the same thing that other famous scientist in the wheelchair had?"

"Yes, but Dr. McCoy has a form that is very rare and is now rapidly progressing as we understand it. We've provided him with resources and equipment since he left so he could continue to work as a hobby as he felt able. I believe he's on the verge of a breakthrough that could really be a financial boon if we could get our hands on it."

"Again, how exactly do I fit into this?"

"Dr. McCoy is now in a wheelchair and getting more immobile by the day. We have sources that tell us he may not have much longer. My plan is to send you in to take care of him and gain his confidence. Maybe then you'll be able to find out what he's working on. You have enough talent and experience to be able to pick out clues once you get inside."

"Why not just ask him?"

"He's developed a very unhealthy distrust of most

people. Especially if they come from this company He won't tell us a word about what he's doing or let us in his house."

"And what makes you think I'll be able to get inside when you've failed?"

"You're going to pose as someone from a home care agency, not someone from the company, like we've tried in the past. I've taken the liberty of calling the agency and canceling their services, so he'll be expecting someone to be showing up from them. That's where you come in."

"Isn't that kind of dishonest?"

"After listening to everything I've just told you, I don't think you really want to jeopardize your career at this point by questioning me, do you?"

"Is that a threat?"

"No one is irreplaceable. Not even you. I don't think you're ready to be looking for another job yet either, are you?"

He could tell by the look in her eyes and the tone of her voice this was an argument he wouldn't get the better of. His mind raced, wondering if it was time to walk away and start a fresh life somewhere else or join in with this scheme. His curiosity won the inner battle.

"It's against my better judgment…but I'll do it."

Her eyes narrowed in an almost evil glare as she looked down at him from across the desk. "You'll be glad you did."

2
MEET DR. MCCOY

The suspension on the old sedan squeaked in protest as Ted brought it to a slow stop and parked along the curb in front of Dr. McCoy's house. The house itself was quite unassuming, no different than any other on the street. He could see the lawn was well kept, probably at the orders of Ms. Wilson. The door to the car made a loud scraping noise as he opened it to get out. This car was definitely several steps down from the BMW coupe he usually drove, but Ms. Wilson made sure every detail of his cover matched up. A low-paid caregiver simply would not be driving around in a BMW. There were butterflies dancing around in his stomach as he walked up the sidewalk to the front door. He didn't let on to Ms. Wilson he had heard many stories about the legends of Dr. McCoy and all the advancements he discovered. In fact, it was when he was reading about one of McCoy's breakthroughs in brain surgery in high school that he decided he would attend the very same university as Dr. McCoy, walk in the same places, and try and gain some of the same knowledge. It was even the reason behind going to work for Pantheon

Inc. so he could work at the same place. Now he was only a few mere feet from reaching the man's front door and meeting him in person. It was time to take a deep breath and prepare to knock on the front door and meet the legend.

"Identify!"

The voice caught Ted by surprise and left his hand hanging in mid-air before it could make contact with the front door. After the momentary shock, he looked around and discovered he was being watched from a security camera off to the side of the door. He turned his face directly towards the camera.

"Hi! My name is Ted Crosby. I'm here from the Willow Brook Home Care service. I'm here to help you."

"I don't need any magazines. Go away."

"Sir, I'm not here to sell magazines, I'm here to help you with your daily needs."

"I don't need any life insurance. Good-bye."

"I'm not selling insurance, I'm just here to help you."

"I don't want any Girl Scout cookies. Besides, you don't look a thing like a Girl Scout."

"I'm not selling Girl Scout cookies, sir, I'm from the care service."

"That's a shame, I'm starting to crave those ones with the peanut butter in."

"If I get you some cookies, can I come in?"

"No, I don't need another newspaper subscription."

"Sir, do you suffer from hearing problems? Can you hear me?"

"Yes, I can hear you now. I don't have any need for a new cell phone. Move along."

"Sir. I'm just here to help you, nothing more, nothing less. May I come in, please?"

This time, his reply was only met with silence. No sound of any kind came from the camera. He tried knocking on the door, but there was no answer. He turned and sat down on the stoop, wondering what he should do next. He had really wanted to meet Dr. McCoy, so he was very disappointed, but he also didn't want to return to the wrath of Ms. Wilson. He picked up a stone on the sidewalk and casually tossed it towards a flower in the yard. His aim was no better with the rock than what it was with his waste paper basketball.

"Pick it up."

Ted turned around to face the camera.

"Yes, you. Pick it up!"

Ted just shrugged his shoulders. He figured he may as well play along with the charade and went over and picked up the stone he had just thrown.

"Put it in your pocket. That's your souvenir."

By now, Ted was really convinced the old guy was completely off his rocker. He put the stone in his pocket anyway.

"What are you doing out there? I thought you were here to help?"

Ted's jaw dropped when the front door opened before him. After the exchange they'd just had, he wasn't totally sure he wanted to go in now, though. Between the craziness of the old man, and the total darkness beyond the doorway, he was really starting to think it might be time to consider a different profession. Against his better judgment, he slowly walked back up the sidewalk and stepped inside the doorway. Before his eyes could become adjusted to the dim light, the door slammed shut behind him, leaving him in total darkness, unable to see.

"Uh, hello? Are you there? Is anybody there?"

"If a tree falls in the forest, but you can't see it, will you still get a splinter when it lands on you?"

"You know, I didn't want to say it before, but you're crazy, old man. Crazy."

"You think you know me so well, do you?"

"You're nuts. What else is there to know?"

Bright lights suddenly came on. Ted was momentarily blinded by the sudden change, but he was aware of something moving toward him from the other side of the room, His eyes adjusted just in time to make out the form of an old man in a motorized wheelchair coming to a stop just inches from him.

"So you really want to know what else there is to know?"

Ted was expecting to see a deranged lunatic looking at him, but much to his surprise, the old scientist's eyes showed a knowledge and depth Ted wasn't expecting. It was almost as if a superior being was looking at him.

"Um, you have secrets, old man?"

The old scientist started making laps around him in his wheelchair.

"What makes you think I have secrets?"

"That's it. You are crazy."

"You're here to do a job. The kitchen is over there behind that wall. Make me something to eat and we'll see about this thing you call crazy. Maybe we'll see if you're worthy to learn of my secrets."

"So you do have secrets?"

"Only to those not in the inner circle."

"Inner circle?"

"I have a craving for scrambled eggs. Let's see what you can do."

Ted's mind was starting to swim with the thought of the secrets Dr. McCoy might have to share after all. Certainly there must be more to this crazy old man than what he was seeing or Ms. Wilson wouldn't have gone to all the trouble of making up this elaborate plan to spy on him. He thought it best not to question any more on this day and try and gain just a little trust with Dr. McCoy.

McCoy watched Ted intensely as he found his way around the kitchen to make the eggs. It felt like his eyes were following every move like it was some sort of test. A test he felt he had to pass. Neither of them spoke as the eggs were cooking. McCoy just sat there, watching Ted's every move silently with great intensity. So great that it made Ted feel very uncomfortable. If not for his inner curiosity of wanting to find out what McCoy might be hiding, he would probably have just walked out instead.

The rest of the evening went quietly, with every comment Ted made to the old man being met with silence. The old man quietly ate his eggs and watched intently afterward as Ted cleaned up the table and washed and dried the dishes.

"Will there be anything else, Mr. McCoy?"

The old man didn't say a word as he powered his wheelchair towards the door and pressed a button on his wheelchair to open it.

"So I'll be seeing you tomorrow, then?"

The old man nodded at him quietly and without a word, closed the door behind him.

Ted walked quietly back to the car, pondering in his mind everything that had taken place. The old man was a whole lot crazier than he would have ever imagined. The only thing that seemed out of place was the mention of "secrets" and the "inner circle." He wasn't sure what any of it meant, but he suspected Ms. Wilson had an idea about it or he wouldn't have been sent on this mission. It all seemed so wrong, but yet all the legends of Dr. McCoy's brilliance left him full of a curiosity driving him to continue. Just at that instant, his cell phone started to vibrate, telling him he had just received a text message. It surely had to be Ms. Wilson waiting for a report and a quick glance at the small screen of his phone confirmed it. He was tempted to ignore it, but he pushed the button to accept the call anyway.

"This is Ted."

"Well? What did you learn? Did you see what he was working on? Does he trust you?"

"You, Ms. Wilson, sent me on a mission to be abused by a raving lunatic. The man has lost his marbles."

"No hints of anything? No evidence of research lying around?" Her voice was starting to get louder and more shrill with each question.

"Other than mentioning some sort of secret and some sort of inner circle, the guy totally freaked me out with how crazy he is."

"I need you to go back again."

"Really? Do you really think there's a need for that?"

"I can't take a chance. If he mentioned there may be a secret, you may be able to find out what he's been working on."

"Okay. I'm willing to give it one more shot. If he's still a nut, I'm done."

"We'll see. You just may be *done*." The chilling tone of her voice turned his stomach. There was no doubting her hidden meaning the way she hissed the word "done" at him.

3
THE REAL DR. MCCOY

Ted's head hung with a feeling of dread as he approached Dr. McCoy's door again the next day. He could think of so many other things he'd rather be doing instead of showing up on this particular doorstep again. He barely slept at all the night before, spending the whole night analyzing everything that had happened the evening before and none of it made one bit of sense to him. He was fully expecting another day of insanity followed by unemployment after disappointing Ms. Wilson by not being successful. He was so lost in his thought that he actually jumped when the door opened before him. His mouth dropped open when he saw Dr. McCoy sitting before him, this time his eyes looking so lucid and full of knowledge it was a little unsettling.

"So how did your report to the great Dragon Lady go?"

"Uh…what? What do you mean?"

"Your boss, the not-so-delightful Ms. Olivia Wilson."

"How…how did you know about the report?"

"Get in here. We'll talk."

Ted stepped inside not knowing what to expect. This

time he was wary of tricks like the day before, so he was prepared for anything McCoy would throw at him. Instead, the old man just motored his wheelchair into the room ahead of him. As soon as Ted was completely inside, the door had closed automatically behind him. Ted was starting to have the sensation of being held prisoner.

"Follow me, please."

The old man quietly drove his wheelchair down a hallway in the opposite direction from where they had been the day before. Ted could see an open doorway up ahead and that appeared to be where they were headed. Once inside, Ted looked around, half curious about his surroundings, and half afraid the room was meant to be his cell. The room itself didn't look threatening, having more the appearance of a den instead of a jail cell. One of the walls was stuffed full of what appeared to be medical and mathematical journals and text books. Next to that was a work table covered with drawings, schematics, and stacks of hand-written notes. Ted was speechless.

"Now, son, just what did you tell Ms. Wilson?"

"Uh...I told her you were crazy."

"Is that all?"

"I said you mentioned something about secrets and an inner circle."

"Excellent!" The old man's eyes were starting to shine.

"Sir? I don't understand."

"I know Ms. Wilson's intentions. Now I must know of yours. Why did you take this assignment?"

"It was assigned to me."

"Is that all? The only reason?"

Ted looked at the floor and thought carefully before answering. "I studied and admired your work while I was in college. I was curious about what you were really like."

"Have you liked what you've learned so far?"

"To be honest, I'm more confused than anything."

"And did Ms. Wilson share with you what she was after?"

"No, sir, she did not."

"Did she tell you why I left the company?"

"I assumed it had to do with your...um...your condition."

"I can see your confusion in your eyes, son. Would you like an explanation?"

"Well, yes. This is all incredibly confusing to me." Ted looked into Dr. McCoy's eyes and suddenly realized there hadn't been a single sign of the crazy man from the day before since he arrived.

"Have a seat, son, this may be much deeper than you imagined."

Ted sat down at a chair next to the work table. He couldn't help but notice right away he was on the same level as Dr. McCoy, not seated below him like Olivia Wilson had done.

"Ted Crosby. Graduated from university near the top of your class. Very gifted, showing far more talent than anyone else in your class. Idealistic, yet trapped in a job that is beneath your abilities and working for the tyrannical Ms. Wilson."

"It sounds like you know me pretty well."

"One of your professors, Dr. Greaves, was a good friend of mine and told me about you. I've followed your career to see what you'd do with your gifts."

"I remember Dr. Greaves. We used to call him 'Papa Greaves.' As far as doing something with my gifts, as you call it, I'm afraid I've not done very much to this point."

"Would you like an opportunity to perhaps change that?"

Ted's eyes widened. "Yes sir, I would!"

"I may be able to do that for you. Provided you agree to be in allegiance with me, and not Ms. Wilson."

"I already don't consider myself to be in allegiance with her. Something about her makes my skin crawl."

Dr. McCoy laughed heartily when Ted said that. "That my son, is a sign of your wisdom! Something that will come in handy if you agree to join me."

"I'd still like to know, is there more behind why you left the company? And how do you know so much about Olivia Wilson?"

"Ted, the main reason I went to work for Pantheon Incorporated was because the original owners allowed me to research in the manner I wanted to without much interference. To do things the right way. I didn't feel exploited and they made a great deal of money from my projects. All that changed when Olivia Wilson joined the company. She made it more about the profit margin. Everything became cold and heartless. But still, I was content to do my research, always trying to learn more. Then one day, all that changed."

"Changed? In what way? What happened?"

"It was while I was in the depths of my research to deal with the repair of nerve damage and spinal injuries I discovered...and I'm not sure how you'll take this...I learned for all the knowledge, all the research, all the wisdom I possessed...we are designed by One so much higher than us, so much more intelligent. And the intelligent One cares for the creatures He designed."

"Are you saying you found religion? That's sure what it sounds like to me."

"Bah! Religion is a waste! I found God, the Creator of all."

Ted was starting to feel things were going to the crazy side again.

"Ted, I can tell from your face, you are skeptical of what I just said. And that's alright. If you make the same discovery, you'll have to take your own path to it. I think your thirst for knowledge will be enough to keep you interested for now. Anyway, when I professed my newfound faith to Ms. Wilson and told her I could no longer perform any more of her unethical tasks...well, you can imagine her reaction."

"Oh, yeah. I bet the veins on her neck really jumped."

Dr. McCoy laughed. "Yes, yes they did. But I couldn't tell what made her madder, my newfound faith or her mental image of all the money she was going to make from my research evaporating before her eyes."

"I'm sure it was a combination of both."

"Probably. Anyway, I've continued my research on my own since leaving the company. My disease has now made it impossible to go any further without help. Before answering if you want to join me, I must confess, I orchestrated your hiring at Pantheon so I could learn what kind of person you've become. I still have friends on the inside that tell me things I want to know. I also worked behind the scenes to get Ms. Wilson to send you to me. You are my choice to help me with the work I have yet to do. I must warn you, we'll have to do some things, extra things, very out of the ordinary, things that may even seem wrong at times, but it will be all necessary for the sake of our research. Now I need to know. Will you help me and keep Ms. Wilson off my back? Or do you owe your allegiance to her?"

Ted had butterflies dancing all through his stomach, just like when he was first meeting McCoy. This time, he was trying to play it cool, but the chance to work side-by-side with the legendary Dr. McCoy was something he wouldn't even consider turning down at any cost.

"Sir, I'm with you."

Ted stuck his hand out for a handshake to seal the deal. McCoy took it in his own, smiling widely as he shook Ted's hand.

"That's great, Ted! I suspected you would be. That's why I brought you to this room."

"You mean to show me your research here?" Ted assumed this was about the notes lying on the work table.

"No. This." McCoy pushed a button on the arm of his wheelchair, activating the bookcase to move to the side and reveal an entrance to the elevator behind it. "Come with me."

Ted followed Dr. McCoy into the elevator. He was still amazed by everything that was happening. He was even more amazed when the elevator door opened at the level below. Inside the lower room was a fully functioning laboratory filled with many pieces of complex equipment, all of them ablaze with flashing lights and LED screens.

"Welcome to my world, Mr. Crosby."

Ted's eyes were full of wonder as he gazed around the room at all the equipment. This was the kind of thing that he used to dream about, what he lived for.

"Sir, I am humbled you trust me to be a part of this."

"Ted, like I said, I've had my eye on you for some time. I figured you'd be a kindred spirit of mine and agree to all this. I must warn you, though, this could be dangerous. There's no telling what Ms. Wilson will do if she gets any sort of idea what's going on here, no telling what she'd have done to you or me. That's why I must also share with you...this room is booby trapped. If you or anyone else tries to do anything here without my guidance, the equipment will self-destruct. In the event of something catastrophic, the whole house will go up in flames in a matter of minutes. Are you still in?"

Ted didn't have to think twice. "Yes, sir, I'm in. All the way."

"Good. We'll start tomorrow. Be here after dark. Now let's get out of here."

Ted couldn't sleep at all that night.

4
PART OF THE PLAN

Ted didn't know what to expect as he walked up the sidewalk to Dr. McCoy's house the next night. But it was obvious the scientist he once thought to be stark, raving mad had a plan in mind. It was also obvious he was expected since the door opened as he came close.

"Welcome, Ted, come right in!"

"You've been expecting me, I see?"

"We have much to do. Much to see. We must be going."

"Going? I just got here!"

"Exactly. You're here, so you can drive. Come along."

Just like before, the door shut behind Ted as soon as he entered. No matter how many times he saw it happen, it was always impressive to see how everything in the house seemed to be operated off of the keypad on Dr. McCoy's wheelchair. Ted followed Dr. McCoy down a hallway in the house. Yet again, McCoy punched a button on his keypad and a door leading to the garage opened before them. There was only one vehicle in the garage, a van that obviously had special equipment installed to handle McCoy's wheelchair.

"Wow, that's quite a ride you have there, Dr. McCoy."

"Please, Ted, we've got a lot of work to do ahead of us. Just call me Carter."

"Okay...um...Carter. Where are we heading?"

"Climb aboard, I'll tell you where to go."

Ted got into the driver's seat as McCoy loaded himself up using the ramp on his side of van. He obviously had done this many times before because he was all fastened in, waiting for Ted to get his seat belt situated.

"Anxious to go are we?" Ted couldn't resist poking a little fun at McCoy's haste.

"I don't mean to rain on your parade here, kid, but realistically speaking, I don't know how much more time I have left on this planet. And there's still a few things I want to accomplish. And I'd be willing to bet one of the reasons you're willing to be a part of this adventure is because you want to accomplish something and make a difference instead of being a corporate shill. Now can we get going now?"

"Well, pardon me for slowing you up."

McCoy laughed. "Turn right at the end of the driveway."

"Your wish is my command."

Just like everything else, Dr. McCoy opened and closed the garage door with the push of a button. After making the requested right turn at the end of the driveway, Ted drove cautiously down the road before them. He was expecting to hear more directions, but instead, they continued traveling into the city. The further they traveled, the worse their surroundings became. At the beginning, the homes were carefully maintained, then the buildings started showing signs of neglect, until the neighborhood they finally ended up in mostly consisted of abandoned and boarded-up buildings. Ted was starting to get a little uncomfortable with their surroundings.

"Turn left at the light ahead."

"You know, we're not in one of the safest parts of the city, Dr. McCoy."

"Carter. And I'm well aware of where we're at."

"This area doesn't make you nervous...Carter?"

"Please, son, I'm old, don't have much time left...and although it doesn't look that way...quite heavily armed."

"I should've known."

"Okay, there's a small gravel road in about a block. Turn right on it."

Ted's senses were working double-time as he pulled onto the gravel road. They were in the seediest part of town and pulling onto a small, dark road and all his best instincts told him this was not a safe place to be.

"Okay, now park by that tree over there on the left."

Now they were becoming a stationary target in a bad area. Ted was really getting nervous.

"Dr. Mc...um...Carter, are you sure it's a good idea for us to be here?"

"Yes. It's part of the plan."

"Plan?"

"Yes. You have to see."

"See?"

"Yes. Look down there. The show's about to start."

Ted looked to an area downhill from where they were sitting. It was dark, but the area was dimly lit by an assortment of candles, lanterns, and campfires. Studying the scene before him, Ted realized what was down below was an encampment of homeless people. The more his eyes grew accustomed to the darkness, the more he could see. There appeared to be about a dozen different people visible, probably some more inside the tents and boxes cobbled together from scraps. He couldn't quite tell for sure, but it looked like one of them was roasting a rat on a stick over a campfire. There seemed to be a quiet desperation that hovered around the encampment, one he could make out on the blank expressions on all of their faces. The overwhelming feeling of hopelessness seemed to be all around. In the midst of all that despair, he became aware of a sound in the distance that seemed to be getting louder, meaning it was heading their way. It was only a matter of seconds until he could identify the sound of an approaching car. In just a few more moments, he could see the car coming, some sort of sports car, a convertible, and it appeared to be filled with a raucous bunch of young men. The homeless people must've been familiar with these people, because they started to run and hide before the car arrived. Several of the young men jumped out of the car before it had even come to a complete stop. Ted could see they were all armed with baseball bats which they used to start attacking all the tents and structures of the encampment. The driver of the car got out, with his bat on his shoulder. Ted shuddered as he saw the young man approaching a couple of the homeless people who had not run off. Ted could only guess there was some reason preventing them from running off like the others. He could see one was lying there, not moving and probably passed out, but the other appeared like he was trying to get up, but was unable. The young man patted his bat several times and it looked to Ted like he was smiling. Ted looked on in horror as the young man took a step back, obviously to build up momentum for his swing, no doubt meant for the helpless man before him. Ted glanced at Dr. McCoy next to him, looking for signs of the same dread he was feeling, but McCoy's eyes were locked on the scene playing out before them, his face seemingly void of emotion. Ted turned back, getting ready to cover his eyes so he wouldn't have to watch, when out of the shadows roared a motorcycle, driven by a rather large man and aimed right at the young man with the bat. Ted could hear him calling out to his friends, who came running to his aid, all of them with their bats ready for battle. The large man calmly brought his motorcycle to a stop, set the kickstand, and slowly got off the motorcycle to face the young men. Ted could hear the young man yelling fiercely, the bat held with menacing authority. He couldn't believe what he was seeing, so he rubbed his eyes and looked again. The large man was smiling at them. Alone, outnumbered, with no weapons and the man was smiling like there was no threat at all. The leader stepped forward and swung his bat, but the big man moved forward as quickly as a cat and caught the bat in his large hand before it could even make it to mid-swing, causing such an opposing force the young man lost his balance and fell to the ground. The big man twirled the bat around and now had it in his hands, still smiling. Ted expected the others to gang up on the big man, but instead, they all timidly retreated to the car and sped off. It appeared they had tangled with the big man before and didn't think they had a chance. As the car disappeared in the distance, Ted watched as the big man helped the homeless man get comfortable again and began to clean up the mess that had been made. After a few minutes, he appeared to be satisfied with how everything had settled out and got back on the motorcycle and rode off, waving to the few people that had wandered back.

Ted was still having trouble believing everything he had just seen. "Is this what you wanted me to see?"

"Part of it."

"You knew this was going to happen?"

"Not totally certain, but the odds were in favor of it happening."

"But how did you know?"

"I've been coming down here fairly often over the last few years. Always seems to be a bunch of young hooligans who want to bully those least able to defend themselves. A couple years ago, the big guy started showing up to protect them now and then. Sometimes his kid comes along and preaches to the people in the encampment. Fascinating people."

"You speak as if you know them."

"Actually, I do. I met them during the course of my other research some time ago."

"Other research?"

"We'll get into that later. Right now, we have something else to watch out for."

"After all this, there's more?"

Dr. McCoy's voice had a solemn and ominous tone in his reply. "Our night is just getting started."

Ted glanced over to McCoy to try and get a read of what was going on inside his head from looking at his face. The old man just sat there stone-faced, looking intently on the encampment below them.

Ted's mind was full of swirling thoughts, unsure what any of this was going to bring about when he saw a pair of headlights approaching. A quick glance towards McCoy confirmed his suspicions. The old man was sitting up a little straighter, his gaze fixated on the approaching vehicle. As it pulled up to a stop, Ted could see it was an expensive sports car, not the type one would expect to see in a run-down area like this. The door of the car opened and out stepped a young man, dressed in clothes that were as obviously expensive as was the car. The homeless people scattered at the sight of the car, obviously recognizing this apparently unwelcome visitor. Everyone was gone, except for the same homeless man who was unable to escape the first attack. Ted's eyes were searching the streets for a sign of the big guy, hoping he'd come back to defend the homeless man again. Ted's concern for the homeless man turned to horror as he saw the young man get something that looked like an aluminum baseball bat and start walking towards the helpless man. It appeared he meant to give him a beating!

"That's our cue."

"What?" Ted was in a state of shocked disbelief.

"You heard me. Drive down there now. We're here to stop the violence this time. Get us down to the homeless man."

Ted reluctantly started the van and drove down towards where the homeless man was sitting. He was starting to get just a little scared, wondering what kind of trouble McCoy was getting them into. The young man saw them coming and didn't appear to be intimidated at all by the sight of the approaching van. Ted was already imagining the morning headlines, telling everyone the story of his demise, when they came to a stop. McCoy was already pushing buttons and opening the door to the van before the tires quit rolling.

"You there, young man!"

Ted watched as McCoy fearlessly exited the van and aimed his wheelchair towards the young man.

"Go away, old geezer! I've got work to do."

"Work? What kind of work do you intend on performing here?"

"Cleaning up the neighborhood. Now leave, or you could become part of the trash yourself."

Now Ted no longer had any doubt in his mind the young man intended on beating the homeless man, maybe even killing him.

"Are you sure I can't talk you out of this?" McCoy calmly spoke to the young man, no signs of fear at all.

"Last chance, old man. Leave now, or there will be consequences you won't be happy with."

"If that's the way you feel about it. Consequences there shall be."

It happened so fast, Ted wasn't even sure what he had seen. It appeared as if something shot out from McCoy's wheelchair and hit the young man. Whatever it was, the young man went down unconscious in an instant.

"Okay, Teddy boy, it's your turn now."

"Uh, what?"

"Your turn. Load this impolite young man into the back of our van if you would. He's a bit too much of a load for me."

"But you….but what…"

"You heard me. Load him carefully, we have to save room for another esteemed passenger."

"Another what!!!!???"

Ted was in shock. He couldn't believe what was happening. As he started to drag the young man towards the van, he watched as Dr. McCoy drove his wheelchair over to the homeless person. He could tell he was talking to the man, yet it was in tones so soft that he couldn't make out any of the words. Then he noticed McCoy hitting a button and watched as the homeless man slumped over where he was sitting. Evidently he would be the other passenger McCoy was talking about.

"Ted, treat this gentleman with a little more care. He deserves it."

Ted could only nod. This whole scene was so surreal it was hard to believe it was actually happening. Having finished loading up the young man, he started to work on loading up the homeless person as McCoy loaded himself into the van. Even though he was still dead weight, he was much easier to work with than the younger man. His body didn't weigh much, and the bulky military jacket the man was wearing probably made up a large portion of the weight. By the smell of him, filth probably made up a sizable portion of the weight as well. Ted carefully placed the homeless man next to the young man in the back of the van and closed the hatch door. He paused to take a deep breath, looking up at the stars above to try and gain a measure of sanity before getting back into the van again.

"Well, you certainly took long enough. I'm sure this isn't what you were expecting, though, so it's alright."

"Sir, I admit at the start I had no idea what to expect. What has just taken place was the absolute farthest thing from my wildest imaginations. I am totally stunned."

"I warned you at the beginning you may have to do some things out of the ordinary."

"Ordinary is not in the same galaxy as what we've just done."

"Maybe not, I'll give you that, but if you stick with me, I think you'll see some things that will make this evening seem very mundane."

"I can't even comprehend that. Not at all. Are those guys still alive back there?"

"Don't worry, Ted, they're both unharmed and under the influence of a special tranquilizer I developed specifically for just this purpose. If you can take it, I think you will see some things that will twist your concepts of reality. I chose you because I thought you'd be up to it. Keep your mind open, because like I've said before, I'm not sure how much time I have left and I need to move fast. I'm not expecting you to grasp it all, just do as you're told and lend a hand."

Ted was torn. This was all very mind-numbing and part of him wanted to jump out of the van and run away as fast as he could. But there was a bigger part of him that wanted to push the envelope of his understanding. He didn't know where this was heading, but the lure of the unknown was more than he could walk away from. He just nodded quietly to McCoy and drove back to McCoy's house without saying another word. McCoy also remained silent until they reached the house.

"Back the van into the garage. It will be easier for you if you stay on the right side."

Ted nodded and began backing the van into the driveway. Of course, McCoy had already activated the garage door so Ted didn't even have to pause as he backed the van into place. McCoy had the door closing as Ted was backing in, so the garage door was fully closed almost simultaneously when the van came to a full stop. McCoy was immediately in motion and was out of the van before Ted.

"Step lively, you still have work to do."

Ted quietly obeyed and made his way to the rear of the van and opened the hatch.

"Okay, now what?"

McCoy pushed a combination of buttons on his control panel. Ted's mouth dropped open as the shelves on the rear wall slid aside to reveal a freight elevator, much larger than the other elevator they had used before. He could see there was a plan in place here, because two gurneys were waiting in the elevator, obviously meant for the two people they had just brought home.

"Get them unloaded and onto these gurneys. Then use those straps to secure them. Tight enough to secure them, but be careful not to cut any circulation off."

Ted got both of the men loaded onto the gurneys, taking care to center their bodies before strapping them down. Ted was thankful the gurneys were like those used on ambulances so the adjustable height made the task of getting them loaded up much easier. McCoy nodded his approval as Ted worked, without saying a word.

"Well, boss, the packages have been wrapped, now what?"

"Ted. Never call me 'boss.' We're colleagues, partners in this endeavor."

"Okay, partner, what's next?"

"Push the gurneys into the elevator. Then your job for the night is done."

"That's it?"

"Yes. I have more work ahead of me to prepare for our task tomorrow."

"Tomorrow? How much longer are you going to keep these guys on ice?"

"The sedative we're using is very easy to customize to our needs. I developed it so something like this could be done long term, if necessary, without causing any harm to the subjects. You'll see."

"Does this mean I'm part of your 'inner circle,' one of the elite?"

"Ted, my boy, it's hardly a circle. At least not yet. For now, it's just you and me."

"For now?"

"I'll tell you what you need to know, when you need to know it. Right now, this is all you need to know. I'll tell you more tomorrow, and more instructions will follow."

"There's nothing more for me to do right now?"

Go home, Ted. You can let yourself out. Good night. Come back bright and early tomorrow morning, I should be ready for you by then."

Ted shook his head. "Good night, I guess."

Ted left McCoy's house in a daze, going over everything that transpired that night in his head. He didn't sleep at all that night. It seemed to be becoming a habit of his not to these days.

5
DISCOVERING THE SOUL

Ted was apprehensive about going back to McCoy's the next morning. He half expected to be greeted by the police at his front door when he stepped outside. What he had helped McCoy with the night before was kidnapping, plain and simple. He knew he had agreed to doing things that seemed beyond ordinary, but kidnapping was definitely against the law. Perhaps McCoy really had gone mad. Perhaps it was all a bad dream and everything that happened the night before never really happened. He replayed all the scenes inside his head as he drove very slowly on the way to McCoy's house. He let out a huge sigh as he parked his car in the driveway. He could feel his stomach tighten as he got out of the car. Never in his entire life had he had such a case of nervousness, but then, never in his life before had he been an accomplice to kidnapping. After the activity of the night before, what horrors might lay in wait for him today? The thought of what may have become of the two people he helped kidnap was starting to make him afraid to walk towards the door, to even take another step. He was seriously considering just turning around and leaving when the front door opened up before him, obviously controlled by McCoy. He looked around as he stepped inside. McCoy was nowhere to be found. As he walked back to the hallway where the entrance to the laboratory was, he had a strong feeling every move he made was being watched. Those suspicions were confirmed when he stepped inside the room. The secret entrance opened before him, beckoning him onward. He had only taken a single step towards it when McCoy's voice came from a speaker hidden somewhere in the room.

"Ted, I've been waiting on you. I have to advise you to keep an open mind before you come down. You're about to see and hear things that will be challenging to the way you've always thought and how you view just about everything. If you have doubts you think you won't be able to resolve, now is the time to turn and walk away. I won't think any less of you. This is a huge leap of faith and understanding for me as well."

Ted knew common sense said he should leave. In fact, he even took a step backwards, but he was too entranced by it all now. He had to see what McCoy was so secretive about, what Ms. Wilson was determined to find out. More importantly, Ted wanted to know for himself. He figured there was probably a hidden video camera somewhere in the room, so he nodded as he stepped into the elevator. This time the voice came from a speaker inside the elevator.

"I'm glad you chose to join me, Ted. This will be an adventure beyond our wildest dreams."

The elevator arrived at its' destination in no time, although to Ted it seemed like it took an eternity. When the doors opened, he was met by McCoy, but he could also see flashing lights, computer screens, and all sorts of equipment that wasn't on display during his last visit to the lab. He gazed around the room in wonder of all the technology that surrounded him, basking in an environment he'd always dreamed of being a part of. The feeling of technologically-induced euphoria stopped abruptly when he saw the two people from the night before, still strapped on the gurneys he had placed them on. They appeared to be unconscious, completely motionless, and both had a large number of sensors and probes leading into the equipment that surrounded them.

"Questions, Ted?"

"Sir. This is...this is beyond questions."

"Fair enough. I'll try to explain the background of how this all came to be."

"Does it have to do anything with that faith thing you told me about earlier?"

"Ted, you are a sharp one! Yes, there is a connection there. I told you earlier about my research into nerve repair and spinal cord injuries. I was into the depths of it when I realized how masterfully crafted all the components of the human body are. It's an incredibly meticulous design and there's no way it could've been some sort of accident rising from some kind of primordial soup. I went on a search to find out more if I could. After visiting a few of the local religious establishments, I was getting pretty discouraged and began doubting the whole thing. Then, I heard about a small church over the mountains where some miraculous things supposedly happened. I was intrigued and went and talked to the pastor there and he made everything much more clear to me. He helped me understand things and taught me so much more than you could imagine. Oh yeah, I got to meet that big guy on the motorcycle there too. He's a fascinating individual. The Almighty really worked some wonders with that man."

"The Almighty? Are you saying you 'found God'?"

"Not just God, Ted. With the pastor's help, I also found the Son of God, Jesus. I learned He died for me. Died so there would be more to my life than this existence."

Ted shook his head and was starting to wonder about

all this religious stuff being introduced in this room full of technology. McCoy had his right to believe what he wanted, but it just didn't belong here at all. "And just what does all of this have to do with those two guys there?"

"A little more explanation first. Have you ever heard of Duncan MacDougall?"

"I can't say that I have."

"How about Guillaume Duchenne de Boulogne?"

"Huh?"

"Guillaume Duchenne de Boulogne. He was a French neurologist. MacDougall did some studies and theorized the human soul weighs 21 grams. Duchenne worked on figuring out how facial muscles make different expressions because he believed they were linked to the soul."

"You really believe in souls, Dr. McCoy?"

"Please, please, call me Carter. And yes, I do. It's part of that 'finding religion' thing as you called it. You see, part of what that young pastor taught me was about my soul, how it lives forever and how important it is to take care of it. More importantly, he taught me the importance of not just believing there is a higher power, but to believe the higher power."

"Believe the power?"

"Yes. That was the most important thing to understand. There's a big difference between believing your neighbor exists and actually knowing and interacting with your neighbor, being their friend."

"Interacting?"

"Yes, interacting. That was something I learned from Pastor Carson. The local religious establishments were missing out, just gathering once a week. Pastor Carson taught me the Creator of all wants us to be a part of His family. For us to know Him and Him to know us."

"That's really sounding pretty weird."

"I understand. It wasn't that many years ago I would've agreed with you. Like I told you before, you must take your own path to this understanding, my understanding alone isn't enough. You have to realize it on your own."

"So, just how exactly does all of this tie into what's going on here?"

"It brings us back to the soul, Ted."

"The soul?"

"Yes. I've discovered the soul. Separate from the body."

"You've done what?"

"I've discovered the location of the soul. And how to transfer it from one body to another."

"I'm not sure I can fathom that. Or even believe it for that matter. Just how did you come up with such a thing?"

"You don't have to believe it, Ted. You'll see for yourself as we go on. I can't claim much credit for the discovery. Oh, I danced close to the facts on my own more than once, but it didn't add up until I saw it in a vision. I firmly believe the Creator was the one that gave it to me. Pastor Carson thinks so too."

"Okay, for the sake of argument, I'll just go along with all that. I still don't see what that has to do with these guys here. Are they some sort of experiment or what?"

"Ted, I needed you for your mind. The young man you see there is Tony Bradford. He's brash, extremely arrogant, but also very, very wealthy, having inherited a rather sizable estate. I need him for his hands and his resources."

"You're going to harvest his hands and steal his money?"

"I know it sounds that way, Ted. But I'm believing he will go along with this plan willingly."

"This is all so unbelievable. And I won't believe it till I see it. But what of the old homeless guy? What could you possibly need from him?"

"I'm not really sure. I was led to him through my vision. I'm just trusting there's meaning to the path I'm following."

"You mean you're not even sure what we're doing with him?"

"I have a basic idea. Just the next step. I'm trusting the rest will come when we need to know it."

"Let me get this straight. I'm risking my reputation, my career, my entire future, possibly some jail time, over something you don't even know about?"

"Yes, rather exhilarating don't you think?" McCoy had a mischievous twinkle in his eye when he said that.

Ted had to pause and think about how ridiculous McCoy's last statement was. Ridiculous, yet accurate. This bit of trusting some mythical, unknown force for direction was a bit more than he could stomach, but all the intricate equipment, the obvious genius behind everything set up in the laboratory was drawing him deeper into this plot, even though he didn't know where it was leading.

"Yes. You're right. I'm still thinking this is wrong, but I have to confess, the mystery of it all has me intrigued."

"Good, good. Your world is going to be turned on its' ear, just like mine was."

"You look like you're starting to get excited by all this."

"Oh I am, Ted, I am. I've always been driven by my research in the past, but now I know other things are more important than personal gain. Whatever this path is I've been called to follow turns out to be, I'm sure it will be something miraculous. I'm also excited because there might be a breakthrough in my spinal research in all of this and now I have you to pass it on to. It was always one of my fears, having my best research dying with me. A selfish thing, I know, but I would like to think there will be something left on this planet to show I was here after I'm gone."

"Now there's something I understand. The mundane existence of the corporate world was becoming more than I could bear."

"I've felt your pain, Ted. Now let's channel that pain and get to work, shall we?"

"Lead the way, Carter." For the first time, Ted felt like a bond was forming between him and Dr. McCoy, like they had a common cause.

"I've gotten all the diagnostic leads hooked up to our friends for the procedure."

"What do I do?"

"You'll get to monitor that equipment over there and tell me when all the readings are in the precise place they need to be. But first, I have to wake up the young Mr. Bradford and explain some things to him."

"Explain some things?"

"You'll see. I need to just tweak the medication a tad. Just enough so he can hear and understand what's about to take place."

"I can hardly wait to watch this show." Ted was actually starting to enjoy this. He watched as Dr. McCoy carefully administered a small amount of medication to Bradford.

"Tony? Can you hear me, Tony?"

Bradford remained motionless, but Ted could see his lips move, although he wasn't close enough to hear him.

"Good. Now do you remember that homeless man you've been tormenting? We found a can of gasoline in your car. You weren't planning on doing anything harsh now, were you?"

Again Ted could see Bradford's lips moving.

"Did you ever think what that abuse would look like from his perspective? The pain you were inflicting? Or did you just think he wasn't worthy as a human being? That you'd be doing society a favor by getting rid of the garbage?"

This time it looked like Bradford's lips were moving faster. He was being louder, but the only words Ted could make out was "worthless scum."

"Well, my dear Mr. Bradford, you'll soon get to live out the old slogan of walking a mile in another man's shoes. You, Mr. Bradford, are about to become a homeless man."

With that statement, Ted saw McCoy administer another injection and Tony Bradford was once again silent.

"Carter, did I hear you say what I thought I did? That you're going to make Bradford experience what he was doing to the homeless man!"

"Yes, Ted. I saw it in the vision. This is to be the first soul swap."

"Soul swap? So you really weren't kidding about that soul stuff?"

"No. I'm very serious. I learned that MacDougall's research was really pretty accurate as far as the weight of the soul. What I was shown in my vision was the true nature of it, which is a spiritual energy. Through my research, I found a way to formulate a substance I can inject into the bloodstream allowing me to track that precise energy through someone's body. From there, I learned how to align that rhythm with the soul rhythm in another body. And in the last vision, I was shown how to transfer that energy, much like an electrical current from one body to another. Those green cables you see, those are the ones that will be tracking the soul movement on the monitors you'll be watching. When all the indicators on both screens become green, you'll give me the signal and then with my equipment here, we'll begin the transfer process. The souls will actually be transported through the blue cables."

"And then?"

"And then Bradford will be living inside the homeless man's body and the homeless man will be living in his."

"Crazy."

"I wouldn't say crazy, but I don't have an adjective to describe it. You're about to see scientific and spiritual history, Ted."

"Well, if you say so."

"You don't sound very confident with the process, Ted."

"This is...well...this is just so far from anything I've ever imagined. How do you know something won't go wrong?"

"Ted, there was a day I would've laughed in the face of

such things. If someone told me the same things I've just told you, I would've laughed at them and would write them off as a blathering lunatic. I don't blame you for not believing in any of this. As for something going wrong, I'm doing all this by faith. I ran tests based on my own soul, but this will be the first time two people will be involved."

"Will you be able to live with yourself if this fails?"

"It's not going to fail. I saw success in my vision."

Ted was starting to have second thoughts. He never believed in such a thing as a soul and now he had a man before him who not only believed in the existence of the soul, but was telling him he knew how to move it from one person to another. He wanted to laugh at him, he wanted to run away as fast as he could, but more than anything, he felt there was something at work here far beyond anything he had ever imagined. This was the feeling inside that was keeping him here. That feeling and his ever growing curiosity to watch this process play out whatever the outcome was to be.

"Okay. This is against my better judgment, but I'm still in."

"Good."

Ted watched in amazement as Dr. McCoy buzzed around the equipment. He was moving so quickly, it was if he wasn't disabled at all. He looked at every screen with an intensity Ted had never seen anyone display before. Although he could barely move his hands, the switches and dials were all handled with a rhythm and precision showing the feeble body was perfectly in tune with the mind. Suddenly, strange sounds started to come out of the machine Dr. McCoy was watching. Ted was surprised to hear the strange noises and thought something might be wrong, but McCoy seemed to be intently listening to them as he monitored the equipment.

"What's that sound coming from the machine?"

"Oh, I forgot to mention the song to you."

"Song?"

"Yes. The song. When you break each person down to the atomic level, each single atom emits a sound much like a musical note. What you're hearing is the songs of their souls playing out as the equipment tracks the soul."

The explanation was so incredible all Ted could do was nod. Words were beyond him.

"I'll take it a level further for you. Something that will really be stunning to a scientific man such as yourself."

Ted was finding it hard to believe things could get any more incredible.

"Mind you, this is only my theory, but what I'm seeing here at this moment backs it up. It's a well-known fact that Mr. Bradford is a godless, narcissistic individual. I present to you the homeless man. He's a man of very few possessions, but among those few possessions were a cross around his neck and a tattered pocket Bible in his jacket. I theorize that he is, in fact, a man of faith. When the song of the soul encounters faith, the tune is different. Listen, if you will, and see if you can perceive the difference between these two souls."

Ted listened closely to the sounds coming from the machines. Just as McCoy had said, the sounds were definitely distinctive. One pattern seemed to be upbeat while the other seemed oddly like a funeral dirge. This surely had to be a coincidence, something McCoy wanted to believe.

"Well, Ted, can you pick up on it?"

"Yes, I can tell the two are different. That doesn't really mean anything, though, does it?, I mean, they're two different people, so it stands to reason the sounds would be different, right?"

"Ah, Ted, I can sense your skepticism. And as a man of science, skepticism isn't necessarily a bad thing. But can you guess which tune belongs to which person?"

"I'm guessing the more upbeat rhythm belongs to your man of faith. Are you sure it's not something you wish to believe, making you biased to that hypothesis?"

"Again, Ted, your line of thought is perfectly legitimate. Keep questioning things like that, it will serve you well later. There is one thing I haven't told you yet, though."

"Oh?"

"Yes. I am a man of faith like the homeless man. Our songs have some very similar patterns. The godless man's song only has a very small similarity, something I attribute to our common humanity. The majority of his song doesn't resemble ours at all."

"What are you saying?"

"I don't have any proof, but I believe it's because my soul and that of the homeless man are in tune with the Creator of the universe."

"I'm not sure I can buy that."

"You don't have to right now, Ted. Just observe, learn. Make your own conclusions as you see fit. I only caution you to keep an open mind based on what you see, not the theories you've been taught."

"Huh?"

"I've learned much of what is taught today at the highest levels is based on biased theories, not reality or extensive research. So many are pushing an agenda, not knowledge."

"I won't argue that. I learned early on there were always two answers, the correct answer and the answer the professor wanted."

"Bravo, Ted! You're ahead of the curve! You're just proving the faith I have in you!"

Ted was a little embarrassed by the compliment. "Let's just get on with this, okay?"

"It's close that time anyway. Check the monitors, Ted."

Ted had been so wrapped up in thought, he had forgotten all about the monitors he had been supposed to be watching. Different colored lines were darting about the screens like some sort of video game. The patterns were becoming nearly hypnotic when suddenly the darting lines came together to form a solid green line going vertically up and down both screens.

"Now! I see the green now!

As Ted called out, McCoy flipped a switch on his control panel that brought another larger monitor to life. Ted could hear electrical noises coming from the equipment and he could swear he saw lights flashing around the two men in rhythm to the sounds coming from the machines. The noises and sights he was seeing made him feel like he was in Dr. Frankenstein's laboratory. McCoy's face was lit up like a small child on Christmas morning as all the equipment buzzed and whirled with electronic activity. Then, without warning, it all stopped suddenly.

"We've done it, Ted. It's finished."

Ted had no feelings. The scene he had just witnessed left him totally speechless, unable to respond.

"Snap out of it, youngster, we have to verify the completion of our experiment."

"Um, oh, yeah, I guess we do." Ted still felt more like he was dreaming instead of being a part of reality.

"Watch closely Ted. There could be more lessons to learn here than we realize."

Ted nodded as he watched McCoy adjust the medication as he had before, but this time, he was doing it to the homeless man. It was then he suddenly realized if Dr. McCoy was successful, the homeless man was now Bradford. Ted watched intently as the medication appeared to be taking effect. The homeless man's eyes started to flutter and then open fully. McCoy moved closer as the man's lips started to move. Ted didn't have to move closer to hear the expletives that started to flow from the mouth of the homeless man. It was obvious to him the words were the thoughts of Bradford's, yet the speech wasn't as crisp, each word having a bit of a slur to it.

"Do you hear, Ted? Do you hear? Bradford's in there now! The damage of life done to the homeless man's body keeps the words from being perfect, but it's obviously Bradford in there!"

Bradford still didn't know what had just happened, but that didn't prevent him from continuing to verbally abuse McCoy and push against his restraints.

"What have you done to me, old man? I've lost my strength, but when it returns, I'm going to beat you to a bloody pulp!"

"Ted, our friend here doesn't know what's going on yet. Should we let him in on our little secret?"

Ted was still a little numb, finding it hard to believe what he was witnessing was actually real. He still had enough presence of mind to nod to McCoy, though.

"Brace yourself, Bradford. You're about to understand what I said earlier about walking a mile in another man's shoes."

Bradford only became more agitated as he continued to curse at McCoy and now at Ted. He was becoming even more frustrated by his feeble attempts at fighting the restraints, not yet knowing his fight was being fought with the body of a feeble, old man.

"Time to stop looking at me, Bradford. Turn your head to the right."

Bradford's face, or at least the face of the old man, was contorted in a fierce grimace as he scowled at McCoy, but he still turned his head as McCoy instructed. The defiant, angry look instantly turned to one of surprise and astonishment and finally a shocked glaze as he recognized the body strapped to the other gurney as his own.

"What....what....have you done?" Bradford's words were now weak and shaky.

"What have I done, Mr. Bradford? I think the more proper question is to ask what you have done. By harassing those less fortunate than yourself, you've earned the reward of being one of them. Get a mirror from that desk over there, Ted. Let Mr. Bradford get a good look at the face he'll be wearing."

Ted did as instructed and held the mirror before the face of the old, homeless man, now occupied by Bradford. Ted could see Bradford making a few facial gestures in the mirror to prove the face in the mirror was the one he was operating. When Bradford had no doubt he had somehow been transformed to the homeless man, he began to quiver and quietly weep. The sympathy Ted felt for Bradford took him by surprise as he turned away to wipe some tears welling up in his own eyes, trying to hide the sympathy from McCoy. His effort was in vain.

"No need to hide your feelings, Ted. Empathy for your fellow man is an admirable quality. One I recognized in you earlier. It's something I hope to teach Mr. Bradford here. I know you may find what is going on here to be cruel, and in a sense it is, but it is no less cruel as what Bradford had been doing to the homeless man and his friends. If this little exercise doesn't turn him into a decent man, nothing will."

"And just what does this 'little exercise' entail?"

"We're taking him back to the homeless encampment. Bradford's buddies are due to make an appearance and this time Bradford will get to see what it's like from the other point of view."

"Won't he just run away? Warn them about who he is?"

"You're forgetting one important detail, Ted. The homeless man's body is weak from years of neglect and abuse. Bradford won't have the body and motor skills he's used to. As you've heard, his voice isn't quite up to par either. Just to be sure, though, I'm leaving enough medication in him to basically ensure he'll be helpless."

"So we're going to dump him out and let him be abused?"

McCoy motioned for Ted to follow him over to the other side of the room, out of earshot of Bradford.

"I'm trusting the big man on the motorcycle will be there to save the day. He seems to be led by the Holy

Spirit to be there at just the right time. If I'm wrong, we'll step in, but I hope it doesn't come to that. Anyway, no need for Bradford to think there's any sort of cavalry around to save him."

"If you're wrong? Sounds pretty risky. Especially that 'Holy Spirit' thing. You know I don't believe in those religious stories."

"I know you don't, Ted. And I'm not trying to force my beliefs on you. Just watch and observe and draw your own conclusions. I can't lead you there if you don't want to go."

"Fair enough. Let's get this over with. I won't lie about it, I'm pretty nervous about what we're doing. So what are we doing with the old homeless man while we're teaching Bradford a lesson?"

"He'll remain peacefully in Bradford's body till we're ready to put him back where he belongs."

"You mean we're going to swap them back again?"

"That's the plan."

"And our end game? Where's it all going to lead?"

"I don't know yet."

"What!!?? You don't know yet? Are you just making this up as you go or something?"

"I've only been following the visions I've been getting. Wherever this is to lead, I don't get any more than I need to know at the time. That's just the way it's worked to this point. Whenever I finish a step, I get the next vision."

Ted smacked his palm to his forehead and shook his head. "Great. Just great. I'm jeopardizing my entire career on something you're dreaming about."

"You're free to leave if it scares you too much."

"No. No, I can't leave now. What you're doing is so much more incredible than anything I've ever done at work or school. I have to see this through to the end."

"Yes. Me too, Ted, me too."

Ted just shook his head.

6
IT'S TIME TO WATCH THE SHOW

Ted had a strange feeling in the depths of his stomach as he closed the van door after loading up the body of the homeless man containing the soul of Tony Bradford. Just thinking of the scenario made his head spin. He was there. He saw it. He witnessed it happening. He saw the results. It still seemed like a strange dream, defying reality. So strange, so unbelievable, yet he was right there living it. McCoy was already loaded up, waiting on him to get into the driver's seat and take off, but he couldn't say he was rushing to get to it. And yet, he didn't want to drag his feet. Like any great mystery, he was driven to find out what would happen next, yet his common sense side kept telling him it couldn't be real. Throw in his scientific inquisitive nature and he was helplessly trapped. Trapped as a player in this game. He hardly felt like a player, though, as he climbed into the driver's seat.

"Shall we go, Dr. McCoy?"

"Carter, Ted. Call me Carter. And yes, let's get this show on the road. My calculations tell me the bad guys will be showing up within 15 minutes of us dropping off

Bradford. It's a tight schedule, but enough wiggle room there to prevent any problems."

"Yeah. Wiggle room. Really feeling good about that."

"I understand this must be making your head swim, Ted. It's only my faith in the visions and my research that gives me confidence this will all work out perfectly."

"Yeah. Perfectly. Excuse me while I remain skeptical."

McCoy started laughing really hard. "Ted, my boy, you just keep on questioning things, it'll keep us honest and prove to you there are things beyond old, dried-up educational theory."

The pair laughed together the rest of the way to the homeless encampment. Ted felt much better since the mood was now lighter. Besides, if the authorities were to show up, they'd be dropping a body off, not kidnapping anyone this time. Just the mental image of trying to explain to the police why they were "delivering" a body made him laugh all over again.

"Okay, chuckles, we're here. Time to drop off our passenger. Pull over there where we picked him up."

Ted pulled over near the tent where they had picked up the homeless man. As he got out of the van, he thought it odd none of the man's meager belongings seemed to be disturbed. He thought of the many times in the office when someone left and their belongings would disappear before their seat had even grown cold, people acting just like vultures over fresh road kill. He would never have thought before there would be more honor among these people than the ones he interacted with every day. It made him feel embarrassed to realize he was prejudiced against these people just because of how they lived. Maybe there was something in this that would bring him some validation to ease his conscience over thinking such things about others. He was, however, happy it was easier to unload the homeless man's body than it was to load him up, a fact Ted was very thankful for. He wasn't really used to the physical side of all this body-snatching and transporting of bodies. He was ready for this part of the adventure to be over with. McCoy had put just enough medication into the old man's body so Bradford couldn't do much with it, but he did have enough use that lifting it wasn't totally dead weight like it was when he first loaded it into the van. Bradford didn't have the ability to put the old man's weight on his legs, but it was enough of a help that Ted didn't have to fully support his weight all by himself as he guided the old man to the same spot near the makeshift shelter they took him from and made him comfortable beside it, just like he was when Ted first laid eyes on him. It looked to him like Bradford was trying to protest, but the medication limited him to faint mumbling sounds and feeble movements of his arms. McCoy's years of research and experience definitely had the use of the medications for control down to a science! Ted marveled at how McCoy orchestrated this whole scene as he got back into the van.

"Well done, Ted, well done."

"Thanks, but from where I sit, I can't tell if I did a good job or not. I really don't know what's going on."

"No need to sweat the details, Ted. Just drive us up under the tree where I first showed you what goes on here. It's time to watch the show."

Ted maneuvered the van back to where they were parked the first time they watched the encampment. McCoy was quiet, but Ted could see his gaze was intense and scanning every detail of the scene below. Ted could see Bradford was trying to move, but not having any luck. His lips were also moving, and Ted assumed every expletive imaginable was being formed in Bradford's mind, yet unable to properly escape the old, medication-impaired mouth of the body he was inhabiting. Ted was so engrossed by Bradford's actions he didn't notice the large SUV approaching until it was almost there.

"Get ready, Ted. Looks like we have company, just as I expected."

"Are you sure this is it? This is really happening?"

"I've seen that vehicle before. This is a habit with them, just like the other bunch we watched before. Let's just hope our benefactor on the motorcycle arrives to save the day again so we don't have to."

Ted noticed the first person to exit the SUV was muscular and well-built. "Yeah, I'm afraid they could probably take us in a fight."

"Never underestimate the power of a wheelchair, Ted, but let's hope we don't have to find out. The results might not be pretty."

"Indubitably."

The pair watched quietly as a total of five individuals, two males and three females, exited the SUV. All of them appeared to be young and well-to-do, which stood to reason considering the expensive SUV they occupied. The driver, who appeared to be the leader of the group, walked with a haughty strut towards Bradford. Ted could see Bradford struggling to move without success as the leader approached him. They were too far away for Ted to understand what was being said, but he could tell the words were all hostile. He winced when the leader kicked Bradford in the face. As Bradford lay sprawled helpless on the ground, the others in the group surrounded him and began kicking him. One of the females pulled a piece of chain from her purse and began hitting Bradford with it.

"We've got to do something!"

"Steady, Ted. Not yet. I know this is hard to watch, but Bradford must live it, must know the full consequences of his behavior."

Even as he told Ted to be calm, McCoy himself was starting to feel uneasy. He had watched scenes like this before and had seen the big man come to the rescue many times, but what if he was wrong this time? What fate would Bradford meet if no one was there to save him in time? McCoy's grip on the arms of his wheelchair was tightening. He could feel a lump growing in his throat as the scene below continued to play out. McCoy could see the leader motioning to one of the others to go back to the SUV. He wondered what they might have planned next What he saw the other young man get out of the SUV horrified him.

"Dr. McCoy is that.."

"Yes, Ted. Gasoline. I think they mean to burn Bradford alive."

"We've got to do something!"

The words had barely left Ted's lips when he saw the attention of everyone surrounding the homeless man shifting towards the road. Ted strained to see what they were looking at, but McCoy already knew.

"It's the big man on the motorcycle. Right on cue. Thank God he's coming, because I don't think we'd have been able to get to them in time."

"But there's five of them to just one of him. I know he's pretty big, but shouldn't we be helping?"

"Just watch, Ted. If it's like what I've seen before, the five are the ones that will be needing help."

"You're kidding me, right? I mean, those guys look pretty muscular, even from here."

"Just watch, Ted. Just watch."

Ted still had his doubts, but he was willing to go along with McCoy's instincts. He watched as the motorcycle came to a stop and the big man got off of it. Ted remembered the man was huge from the other time McCoy brought him here to watch, but Ted was still taken aback by the sheer size of him as he dismounted the motorcycle. It was easy to see the females were intimidated, as they instantly backed away from the homeless man and started taking steps backwards toward the SUV, but the arrogance of the young men was on display as they started to strut towards the big man. Ted could hear one of them yelling at him in a threatening tone but they were too far away to hear what was being said. The two young men were now splitting up, obviously knowing their best plan of attack was to gang up on the big man from opposite sides instead of one direction. The big man didn't seem to be too concerned about the impending attack. Ted could see his mouth moving, and from his demeanor, it appeared to be a very non-threatening message he was delivering. Whatever it was he was saying, it wasn't preventing the two young men from getting into position, ready to attack. The mood was so tense, Ted and McCoy both jumped in their seats when the pair simultaneously leaped to attack the big man. Ted was mentally prepared for a vicious fight, but he wasn't prepared for what his eyes were now showing him. The big man caught both of the young men at the same time by the scruff of their necks and tossed them both aside as if they were rag dolls. The one who had appeared to be the leader of the group quickly jumped to his feet to continue the battle while the other one started to retreat towards the SUV without even taking the time to get up off the ground. It was a comical sight to see him scrambling along the ground, much like a crab. The leader ran at the big man, coming in low in an obvious attempt to hit his legs and knock him over. That plan didn't fare so well as his face was met by the big man's foot, he having perfectly timed the assault as if he had known exactly what was coming. The big man didn't seem to put much effort into kicking him, but the contact sent the young man flying backwards at a much faster pace than his forward assault. He landed in a heap, the dust rising up around him in a cloud. The young man shook his head as if to clear his senses and once again got up and ran at the big man, this time swinging his fists. Once again, the big man perfectly timed the assault, grabbing the young man's arm and flinging him aside. The young man still possessed an evil determination, getting up off the ground and charging the big man yet another time. This time, instead of standing still, the big man charged back. The young man stopped in his tracks, the defiant look on his face turning to one of fear. Instead of hitting the young man, the big man grabbed him by his shirt and held him off the ground with his feet dangling below so he was looking him directly in the eyes. Ted couldn't tell what the big man was saying, but he could see a look of terror in the young man's expression. The big man finished speaking to the young man and gently set him back down on his feet. The fear had not left him, evidently, because he just stood there motionless. Ted could see the others in the group had gotten back in the SUV and were calling out for their leader to join them. He was still standing there motionless, his mouth hanging open, his eyes wide with fear. The big man said something else and raised his hand, pointing at the SUV. Whatever he said, it convinced the young man to join his friends and leave, although there was still plenty of fear in him, since he walked backwards the whole way, tripping and falling over twice as he went, not taking his eyes off the big man for a moment. The big man paid no attention and walked over to the homeless man, kneeling down so they were on the same level and speaking to him. Ted could tell from Bradford's feeble body language the big man was comforting him and putting him at ease. Neither of them seemed to notice the SUV speeding away from the scene as fast as it could go.

"Well, Ted, it looks like God took care of this situation just as He had it planned."

"That big guy isn't God."

"No, he isn't. But God is inside him and he lets God direct and use him. Something I'm trying to learn better in the little time I have left."

"Yeah, okay, sure. But what do you suppose the big guy was saying to that young man? He surely didn't seem too excited during those times he was being attacked."

"I've only met the man a few times. But from what little I know of him, I would bet he was telling the youngster about Jesus. From what I understand, he has a habit of doing that when he lifts someone off the ground."

"He was preaching to him in the middle of a fight?"

"Probably. I hope you get to meet him someday, Ted. He's a fascinating individual with stories to tell."

"If you say so. You think Bradford learned his lesson from this?"

"I certainly hope so, Ted. So much depends upon it."

"What do you mean by that?"

"I can't tell you yet. But you'll see. I've seen the next step in my visions, but that's all."

"Wonderful. We're following your dreams again."

"Worked out pretty good on this evening, didn't it?"

That was a point Ted couldn't argue. "Yeah, I guess it did."

Ted suddenly became aware of the big man's motorcycle starting up and the pair of them watched as the motorcycle turned around and disappeared down the same road the SUV had arrived on. Bradford was now by himself again.

"Let's go down there, Ted. It's time."

Ted fired up the van again and drove it down to where Bradford was seated. McCoy was already in motion before the van came to a complete stop. McCoy was moving so fast, he was already beside Bradford before Ted had even closed the door on the van.

"Well Bradford, what was it like to be on the receiving end?" McCoy wasn't wasting any time going after Bradford. Ted could see Bradford's lips moving, but wasn't close enough to hear what he was saying.

"Dr. McCoy, what are you doing?" Ted was puzzled by McCoy's sudden boldness.

"Load him up, Ted. I've a proposal for young, Mr. Bradford once we've returned home. If he accepts, we have much to do."

Ted nodded without saying a word. By now, he was realizing McCoy had a plan in place. The guy didn't do anything without a plan, but what frustrated Ted the most was the plan always revolved around the mysterious visions he claimed to have. Ted was in this too deep to back out now, and besides, he was seeing true genius in the workings of McCoy's laboratory. There was still the potential of learning great mysteries of science from him, potential Ted didn't want to miss out on. The conflicting feelings raged on inside Ted's mind until his thoughts were disrupted by their arrival back at McCoy's.

"Bring him to the laboratory, Ted. I'll meet you there." McCoy's eyes showed a determination beyond what Ted had seen to this point.

"Yes, sir. We'll meet you down below."

Ted could only imagine what awaited down below in the laboratory. After seeing the results of what McCoy called the first "soul swap," Ted felt anything could happen. Bradford was still not capable of much movement, but Ted could sense a more submissive demeanor in him now, as if he were actually trying to help as much as he could. This made Ted happy, since it made lugging him around a little easier. There seemed to be a curious tension in the air as they progressed toward the laboratory. That tension didn't go away when the doors to the laboratory opened. McCoy already had the equipment buzzing, a sure sign to Ted he was anxious to proceed and had more "soul swapping" planned.

"Set our friend up here on the table, Ted."

Ted carefully loaded Bradford onto the gurney just as he had before, being careful to have him strapped down securely. This time Bradford was conscious of what was going on, yet didn't struggle a bit.

"Now tilt the table so we can be more comfortable as we converse."

Ted fumbled with the controls on the gurney until he found the right control to tilt the table. This put Bradford's face on the same level as McCoy's. McCoy wheeled over so his face was close to Bradford's. Ted watched as the two men's eyes met. It almost seemed as if the conversation began before the first word was uttered.

"Ted, hand me the yellow vial from my table over there. It's time to undo some of the medication so we can have a good chat with our friend here."

Ted brought the vial over to McCoy and watched as he precisely measured a small quantity out and administered the drug. The effects were immediate. Bradford began to cry.

"It's okay, Mr. Bradford, you've been through a lot. Let the emotion out."

McCoy seemed to be showing genuine sympathy for this man whose soul he had imprisoned in another man's body and put through an incredible ordeal. Ted was a little surprised, but with everything he'd witnessed, there were no longer any big surprises.

"Whaa..." Bradford was having a little trouble speaking, not yet being used to the damaged body he was in. "Sorry, so...sorry." Bradford started crying again.

"Do you understand, now, the abuse you heaped upon those people?" McCoy gently spoke to Bradford in a tone meant to be comforting.

Bradford continued to cry. "So very...sorry."

"You know you deserve jail for your crimes? To be prosecuted and locked up?"

Bradford was still crying as he nodded.

"Would you be willing to make a deal with me? A deal that gives you a chance to set things right?"

Ted was intrigued by the statement just made by McCoy and listened even more intently to what was being said.

"I want you to think about this offer very, very carefully, Mr. Bradford. It's a very serious offer, not one to be taken lightly. Are you willing to listen?"

Bradford's face showed obvious shock at McCoy's offer. After a few moments, he nodded his head slowly.

"Listen closely, Bradford, so you're sure to understand. Ted, you listen, too. You'll be involved with this as well."

Ted nodded, his curiosity starting to get the better of

him.

"I'm sure you both can see I'm an old man. You can also see my body is very feeble. My time in this world is short. I've been performing research most of my life, and I feel I'm about to make a major breakthrough in the repair of nerve damage and reorienting brain function. I know that probably means little to you, Bradford, but the potential is tremendous. I don't have time to try to sell you on my ability, but consider where you're residing. In another man's body. I don't claim to have come up with the know-how to perform that all on my own, but the whole process is more than you need to know right now. Consider what I've just told you Bradford. Are you ready to hear my proposal?"

Ted could see by the expression on Bradford's face and the look in his eyes, he had been carefully listening to everything McCoy was saying. Ted was hoping this was the case, because he really wanted to hear what the proposal was himself.

Bradford's lips trembled unsurely, still not used to the damaged body, he spoke slowly. "Sir, I never considered the pain I inflicted on others. I'm not sure what you've done, but whatever it was, you showed me how wrong I've been. If you can help me make this right, I'm ready to do anything you say. Anything." Bradford's whole body started to tremble and he started to sob uncontrollably.

"All right then. Here it is. As I said, I'm old. To complete my research may take longer than my feeble body will inhabit this planet. I would like to perform the same transfer on myself and borrow your young body in order to complete my research while I'm still alive."

Ted felt like he was frozen in time, with nothing moving. McCoy's proposal was incredulous to imagine. Would Bradford agree to such a thing? More importantly, what would become of Bradford or McCoy's research if he didn't agree to it? Ted felt like he had more anxiety about Bradford's decision than McCoy did. Ted carefully studied the expression on Bradford's face for clues of what was going on inside his mind. After a few moments of careful thought, Bradford seemed ready to respond.

"I'll do it. This all sounds like something out of a science fiction horror movie, but I'll do it. I deserve far worse for the way I've treated those people. Do what you need to do." Bradford lowered his head and began to cry again.

McCoy moved closer to Bradford and placed his hand on his shoulder. "I promise to do the very best I can to make you proud of your contribution to this endeavor. When we're done, you'll be able to hold your head up high."

Bradford raised his head up till his eyes met McCoy's. There was a smile on his lips.

"I certainly hope so. I certainly hope so."

7
ANOTHER SWAP

"Are you ready Ted?"

McCoy's words brought Ted back to reality. He had been daydreaming about everything that had happened. He was there. Witnessed it all. Yet, it still seemed so bizarre, like a dream. Yet there it all was before him again. Bradford, or at least Bradford in the homeless man's body, and the homeless man, in Bradford's body, were all strapped in and connected to the equipment just like before.

"Pay close attention, Ted. You're going to be running the controls on the next go-round. All of them."

That immediately brought Ted back in complete focus. "Yes sir, I'll watch every step."

"Good. We have no room for error in this endeavor."

It all happened just like before. The sights, the sounds, the eerie music. Ted saw and heard all the same things, yet this time, he could swear that Bradford's "music" had a slightly different tone to it. Ted made mental notes of everything McCoy did along with jotting down a few notes in his notebook along the way. He was determined to be able to perform these tasks to perfection when the time came. He still felt like he was only on the fringe of all this, but there was no way he wanted to let McCoy down, not after all they'd been through to this point. He was so engrossed in the details the sounds of the machines shutting down took him by surprise.

"Looks like it was a success again, Ted!" McCoy exclaimed triumphantly.

Ted watched as McCoy administered the medication to bring Bradford back to full consciousness. He seemed a little groggy at first, but it was only seconds until he seemed fully aware.

"Bradford? Are you feeling okay? Any problems?" McCoy asked the questions, but the tone of his voice reflected the confidence he had in his process.

Bradford looked McCoy squarely in the eyes. "Yes, I feel great. So good it doesn't seem real. If there's a problem, I don't know about it."

"Good, we have work to do."

McCoy looked both pleased and peaceful as he checked his monitors and began disconnecting the equipment leads from the two men. The success of the procedure seemed to energize him and give him new vigor.

"Doc?"

"Yes, Bradford, what is it?"

"Just what is this work we have to do?"

McCoy nodded toward the homeless man. "First, we have to get our friend here back to where he belongs. We have to get him back so we can start our deal."

"Oh. Yeah. The deal."

"Not thinking of backing out of it, are you Bradford?"

"No. I gave you my word. I'll stick to it."

"Good. I didn't think you would back out after what you've been through."

Ted wondered if Bradford actually was going to keep his word. After all, there was nothing here to prevent him from running. McCoy had a lot of tricks in his wheelchair, but Ted doubted the ability to chase someone down was built into it. A ridiculous investment in technology, an insane amount of risk involved, and they were putting it all in the hands of one man's word. A man who neither Ted nor McCoy really knew at all.

"Sir, normally, at least for the person I was, I would bluff my way through this...run away at the first opportunity. But what I've just gone through here, well, I can't quite wrap my head around all of this just yet, but I think I need to change my ways. I just...just feel something different. I can't quite put my finger on what it is."

"You can ponder that on your own time, Bradford. Like I've said, we've still got a lot of work to do." McCoy's matter-of-fact demeanor didn't take any of them by surprise. Nor did the abrupt way he broke off the conversation and continued disconnecting all the leads from the equipment and meticulously arranging them in place on the machines.

Ted watched passively, not really sure what he was feeling inside, as Bradford swung his legs over the side of the table and flexed his muscles. He had been there for this entire technological miracle, seen the whole thing play out, yet inside nothing going on felt real.

"C'mon Ted, snap out of it, we have to get our homeless friend here back to where he belongs." The sharpness of McCoy's voice broke Ted out of his daydream and brought him back to what was happening.

"Sorry, sir, I was lost in thought."

"Enough of the 'sir,' Ted, it's Carter, remember?"

"Yes sir, um...Carter, sir....uh....Carter."

"Get it together, Ted. It's important you and I work closely on this. I believe there are things I am to pass on to you before I leave."

That caught Bradford's attention. "Leave? Are you going somewhere Dr. McCoy?"

"I told you before, Bradford, I'm old, and getting older with every breath. I wish you youngsters would pay closer attention to what I say. Time is precious, you know." The wink McCoy gave them let them know he wasn't totally serious with his scolding words. He even started whistling as he wound up the remaining cables that had been attached to the homeless man and put them in their places on the machine.

"I have our friend cleaned up and ready to travel, boys. Time for you guys to take him for a ride." McCoy reached inside a drawer in the cabinet and pulled out a vial of liquid. "When you have him back where he belongs, give him a shot of this, okay? It will bring him back to normal."

Bradford had a puzzled look on his face. "Is that some sort of magic potion?"

McCoy laughed out loud. "It's hardly a magic potion. A lot of hard work and divine inspiration went into it. Maybe Ted can tell you more during your trip."

Ted was obviously surprised to hear McCoy wouldn't be joining them in returning the homeless man. "Are you sure you won't join us? I doubt I'll be able to answer any questions Mr. Bradford might have."

"I have a few things to prepare here for the next transfer, Ted. I keep learning something new each time. I also want to make sure I have all the instructions you'll need in order. I have a feeling there's something really big at the end of this trail. We cannot...no, we must not...fail. Failure is not an option."

"But what if we fail in returning this homeless man?"

McCoy started laughing. "If you two fail in this simple task, then all is lost! Now get to it! Make me proud!" McCoy began laughing even harder.

"C'mon Bradford," Ted said with an obvious smirking expression. "It's up to us to make the laughing doctor a happy man."

"I thought this was a serious task. You guys seem to be enjoying this." Bradford appeared to be puzzled.

Ted nodded towards McCoy. "He's the one enjoying this. You and I are just along for the ride. He knows what's going on and I have no clue."

McCoy's laughter stopped suddenly as he turned to face them. "Your clues will come soon enough Ted. Soon enough."

The sudden solemn tone of McCoy's voice caught the pair by surprise and left them momentarily speechless.

"Sorry, doc," said Bradford in a very timid voice, "We'll take take care of this as best we can."

Ted sheepishly nodded in agreement.

"Stop looking like someone just kicked your dog, Ted. It's just that I've invested a lot of time in this research and..." McCoy's voice trailed off.

"And what, Carter?"

"Ted, it's...well...I've spent a lot of time studying you, following your career, and now...now that we've worked together for a bit...well, Ted I almost feel like we're family. I know it's only been a short time, but I feel we've bonded. And I have so very much I want to pass on to you before I go."

Ted was stunned. He hadn't thought about it before, but McCoy's words made him realize the two of them had bonded to some extent, in a rather unlikely friendship. In the short time they'd worked together, Ted already started looking forward to the time in McCoy's lab. Now that McCoy had put it into words, it was becoming crystal clear to him a special bond had, indeed, formed between them. The glances of trust and respect passing between them said more than any more words could add.

"C'mon, Bradford, let's get this guy back. McCoy has some important work for us to do." Ted gave McCoy a nod and a wink and began preparing to move the homeless man and the gurney. Bradford jumped in without question and joined Ted on the other side of the gurney, ready to make the return trip. He did his best to show how eager he was to carry out the task at hand.

"Okay, doc, our bags are packed and we're ready to go!" Ted's lighthearted delivery put everyone at ease as the pair wheeled the gurney towards the lab's elevator. "It's getting so we're running out of night and the day will be coming sooner than we know it. You know, I've still got to report back to the dragon lady, so what do you say after we get our friend here delivered back home, we all catch a few hours of sleep and meet back here around mid-morning after I'm done making up some fairy tales for the boss woman?"

McCoy got a very serious look on his face and took a few moments to think over Ted's offer before answering. "You make a good argument there, Ted. That will give us some time to rest up and give me a little more time to get things in order. It should help make everything run smoother."

"Then it's settled! We'll all meet back here tomorrow. And Bradford, I'll pick you up at your place in the morning so our timing is more coordinated."

"Whatever you say." Bradford knew better than to say anything that would conflict with the plans of either Ted or McCoy.

"Alright! Let's get this taken care of!" Ted pushed the button to open the elevator door and wheeled the gurney inside. "C'mon, Bradford! Hop to it!"

Bradford just nodded silently and followed the gurney into the elevator. It was a tight fit, but for some reason it seemed especially cramped this time. The silence in the elevator was awkward as they ascended to the main floor from the laboratory. Neither of them said a word as the two of them easily loaded the gurney holding the homeless man into the van and climbed inside to start their mission. They had only traveled a few blocks when Bradford couldn't take the silence any longer and broke the ice.

"So, Ted. We haven't really gotten to know each other. My name's Tony Bradford. Just how long have you been working with McCoy?"

"Not long. Not long at all."

"Really? Seemed to me like you two had been working together for a long time."

"Yeah. Seemed like a long time to me sometimes, even though it hasn't been." Ted laughed at his own joke.

"So tell me about this dragon-boss lady you were

talking about. There must be a story there."

"Not too much to say really."

"Well, where do you work? What do you do?"

"I'm a research scientist. At Pantheon Incorporated."

"Olivia Wilson!"

"Uh, yeah. That's right. She's the dragon lady. Let me guess, you're her brother or something, aren't you?"

Bradford let out a big laugh at that comment. "No, thank goodness, I don't think I could stand sharing bloodlines with her. It's hard enough knowing we're the same species."

"So how do you know her?"

"I'm sorry to say I run with the same crowd as she does. Although I do try to keep my distance from her."

"Oh, really?"

"Yes. The woman's certifiably a nut case."

"Can't argue that fact. Not even a little bit."

"Say, did you ever see her face..."

"...change from happy-face to evil with no warning? Oh yeah, lots of times."

"You have my sympathy. And I do mean that."

"Well, I gotta say I brought the worst out in her sometimes. Everyone else in the office chose to kiss-up to her. I always had a tendency to speak my mind instead of just talking nonsense to make her happy. Brought the evil face on many a time that way."

"I bet. I always found it entertaining to watch her change personalities to suit her audience."

"Oh yeah, I used to see that a lot. A loyal, hard-working soldier when the company big-shots were around and an evil, slave-driving tyrant when they weren't."

"Ever see the sickening 'chummy' act?"

"Yep. I think sometimes she actually made herself believe everyone liked her when she did that one."

"I feel sorry for you, having to work for her and go through all that."

"There were times I felt sorry for me, myself. I think

the worst was when she was partying with her old college friends all weekend, doing who knows what kind of illicit substances, and showed up Monday morning all hostile, and tripping out on everyone."

"Really? Sounds like a nasty experience."

"Oh, it was. I knew it was trouble when I saw those glazed eyes. She even threatened to rip my heart right out of my chest and then slice me up into little pieces."

"Whoa! That's pretty wicked!"

"Yeah. And to top it off, I got written up for insubordination for trying to break up her little manic episode and make her smile. She was so screwed up on whatever drug she was using, I don't think she even remembered most of the incident."

"I could definitely imagine her doing that. That's why I always tried to keep my distance."

"Can't say that I blame you. Wish I had that option."

"So what's this report thing all about, anyway?"

"She assigned me to spy on McCoy. To learn all about what he's up to."

Bradford suddenly got quiet and somber. "Just what are you going to tell her?"

"As little as possible. I just can't let McCoy down now. This...this is all just so crazy. It all just feels so unbelievable, like it's a dream or something."

"You should see how it feels from where I'm sitting."

"No argument there. Do you believe all this soul stuff McCoy's been talking about? You've been the guinea pig for it. What do you think?"

"I don't really believe in that soul business. Never have. But he's definitely on to something."

"Yeah. He is. It's kind of hard to explain, but I enjoy being on his side. I feel far more loyalty towards him than I ever would for Ms. Wilson. I don't want to do anything to displease him or be a detriment to his work, so I'm just going to make something up to keep her off the trail of whatever it is he's doing."

"I don't even know the guy, but he has to be a step up from,,,what did you call her?...oh yeah, the dragon lady."

"You never did tell me. Just how did you get tied up with Wilson anyway?"

"We were in the same social group, hung out at the same places. I'm ashamed to say the thing we most had in common was our belief we were better than everyone else. And wealthier. Some of us were born that way, others got it dishonestly, or in the case of Wilson, by rising through the ranks using unethical practices."

"You don't seem to be that kind of guy just sitting here talking to you, yet the guy who was about to attack our friend back there definitely seemed to have issues."

Bradford's head lowered and his eyes carried a sad look to them and seemed to become fixated on his shoes and his voice became halting and weak. "I did. I did have my inner demons I constantly battled. I was becoming more and more depressed every day from the life I was living. The only thing that kept me going was abusing those homeless people. I thought as a superior person I was making the city a better place by getting them out of it. I got a momentary sick feeling of pleasure from it, but it always left me feeling empty. Then this thing McCoy did showed me what their world was like. What I was doing to them. Now I don't think I can ever be the same again. I'm hoping I can redeem myself a little here and correct some of the damage I've done."

Ted listened to Bradford's confession with great interest. He prided himself on being able to read people and discern what they were like and Bradford's words seemed genuine enough. Yet, he still couldn't help but remember the evil look he had seen on that same face not that long ago. Part of him still thought Bradford would back out of the agreement and run off as soon as the homeless man was returned. He was soon to find out.

"We're here, Bradford. Kind of surprised to see your car still intact, though. I figured it would be up on blocks with all the windows broken out or something."

"One more night it probably would have been. The only thing that protected it was they were probably afraid of me or one of my friends coming back. People get braver as time goes on. I hadn't thought about it till now, but I don't remember where my key fob for the car is at. A lot has happened in the last 24 hours you know. We'll probably just have to leave the car sitting there anyway."

"Is that how it is for you on this adventure? You're getting braver as time goes on?"

"Well, no, I'm still borderline terrified over what's coming next."

"I'd like to put your mind at ease...but I can't. This is all really...well, I can't put words to what's going on."

"Yeah, I understand. I can't really describe it either."

"There is one thing I can do to put your mind at ease. McCoy gave me your fob. The dude never seems to miss a detail."

"Apparently not." Bradford grabbed the fob from Ted's hand as he dangled it in his direction.

"Well. Let's get to it and get this over with, Bradford."

Bradford nodded and they both got out of the van and went around to the rear, opening the doors. The homeless man was still under the influence of McCoy's special sedative and was easily unloaded. There were no words exchanged between the two of them as they wheeled the gurney to the spot where the homeless man's makeshift shelter stood eerily dark and silent, as if it could tell the essence of the man's soul was not there. Carefully unstrapping him, the two silently exchanged nods as they lifted the man off the gurney and placed him on the ground at the front of his shelter. Bradford paused a moment, entranced by how homey the man had made the entrance to the shelter. The well-worn strip of carpet kept the doorway free from dirt and was surrounded by a variety of cans, each one containing well-used candles, obviously for lighting up the nighttime hours. It suddenly struck him how content these people were with so little when he was so unhappy having so much. That thought was interrupted by the sound of Ted opening up the small medical bag he had brought along. Bradford recognized the vial of medication McCoy had given them.

"You know what you're doing with that thing?"

"Yeah. McCoy gave me pretty strict instructions, and if that wasn't enough, he has another set of instructions printed out here in the bag. Like I told you, that man doesn't miss a detail."

"I thought there'd be a label with instructions on it."

Ted chuckled at that comment. "McCoy made this stuff. If ever there was a genius mad scientist in real life, he's it."

"You mean..."

"Yep. This is his own formula. He made it himself. You should know how well it works. You've had some yourself."

Ted took the hypodermic needle McCoy included in the bag and drew out the precise amount of the formula as instructed.

"Just a slight pinch in the arm, and sleeping beauty here will come back to life. Bradford, if you would, load this gurney up for me so we can get out of here as quickly as possible. The instructions say we have about a full minute before this man becomes fully aware again."

"Will do. Just to clarify, you'll be picking me up tomorrow, right?"

"Yes, that's right."

"Hey, wait a minute! I've never told you where I live!"

Ted pulled what looked like a map from the medical bag and waved it in Bradford's direction. "I told you, McCoy covers every detail."

All Bradford could do was shake his head in disbelief.

"Okay. As soon as I get this thing loaded, I'll head to my car. See you sometime in the morning!"

"Count on it!"

Bradford loaded up the gurney and ran over to his car, hopped in and started it up. He watched and saw Ted was making sure he was ready to leave before injecting the homeless man with McCoy's concoction. Ted quickly injected the medication into the man and rapidly returned to the van and jumped in. The pair of them saluted each other and drove off in different directions. Bradford, however, turned around after a block and went back. He just had to see the results of their night's work. He figured it would be no big deal to park on the hill overlooking the man and watch his recovery. As soon as he doubled back and rounded the corner, he saw he wasn't alone in his thinking. Ted was already there, parked in the van. Bradford pulled his car alongside the van since there was no use in hiding. The pair exchanged a knowing glance, each one knowing the other had the same thought. As they looked below, they saw the homeless man starting to stir. He slowly sat up, looked around and shrugged his shoulders, looking like he had just awoken from a nap. The man then stood up, bent over and entered the short doorway to his makeshift shelter as if nothing had ever happened. Ted and Bradford looked at each other, both of them giving the other an understanding nod, and drove off, this time really leaving.

8

THE DRAGON LADY

Morning came too swiftly for Ted. His sleep that night was fitful. If it wasn't the activities of the night before waking him up in a cold sweat, it was the anticipation of his meeting with the less than delightful Ms. Wilson haunting his dreams. He always hated being around her before and now that he'd been working with McCoy, the last thing he wanted to do was betray any of McCoy's activities or secrets to her. He stared into his morning cup of coffee, hoping it would last for hours so he wouldn't have to leave on his journey to the den of the dragon lady. Unfortunately, the coffee didn't last forever and Ted had to reluctantly begin his journey. His first thought was to try and fly under the radar, blending into the background as much as possible. That thought was shattered when he walked out his front door and was confronted with the reality he had forgotten his car was at McCoy's house and he was still driving McCoy's van. So much for blending into the background. He was still mentally bemoaning the absence of his car as he stopped at the security gate at Pantheon to pick up a temporary parking pass for the van.

"Get a new ride Ted? I sure wouldn't guess you'd pick a van like that thing. Doesn't seem to be your style." Tom, the security guard, was a friendly guy, but Ted wasn't in the mood to be friendly on this morning.

"No buddy, just a one day swap with a friend."

"I think your friend got the better of the deal."

"Yeah, I think you're right."

There wouldn't be any sneaking the van into the parking lot. Not only did it stick out like a sore thumb, he had to park it in the temporary parking area, which just happened to be below the window of Wilson's office. He considered just turning around and calling in sick, but there in the window he saw Ms. Wilson's face, glaring out at the unfamiliar vehicle beneath her window. It was strange, but for the first time in his life, he felt a presence, a distinct presence of evil in the air around him. He felt shivers running through his body as he got out of the van and saw she was still staring at him. He could almost imagine her eyes were glowing red at him too. It was easy for him to dismiss these feelings as a combination of little sleep and all of McCoy's talk of souls, yet there was something about it that felt all too real to him. His movements were slow and deliberate as he moved towards the door and stairs that would lead him to her office. Although it had never been a cheery trip, he just couldn't shake the feeling of darkness all around the building. And it kept feeling darker with every passing step towards the office. He silently cursed McCoy for putting such ideas of "darkness" into his head. It had to be McCoy. Even though this sense of darkness kept getting stronger, there was no way it could be real. Ted wouldn't allow himself to believe what he was feeling was real. What was undeniably real, howeever, was the evil within Ms. Olivia Wilson and he was about to face her. He could see Wilson up ahead in her office. She appeared to be having a meeting with one of the people answering to her who had sold their souls to please her in an effort to move up the corporate ladder. He could see them smiling and laughing. And then, Wilson turned and saw Ted coming down the hall. The happy, smiling face of Ms. Wilson changed as if a sheet suddenly dropped away to reveal another face, a face filled with evil and hatred. The employee took the hint and slipped out of the office as quickly as possible.

"Well, Ted, how are you? It's about time you got back." Her voice seemed to hiss at him even more than usual. He felt a chill in the air around them as she got up and closed the door behind him.

"Well, you know me, always taking time to make sure the job's done right." He played it nonchalant, but he wasn't sure if she was buying his act or not.

"And you know me, Ted. I want results. What do you have for me?"

"Not much yet. Dr. McCoy hasn't made much progress on whatever he's working on. We're still trying to get the equipment to work."

"That doesn't sound like McCoy. He's got a reputation for being efficient and getting things done and also getting the job done in a ridiculously short amount of time."

"He's old, you know."

"Yes, but I have reason to believe his mind is still intact. You should've been more than capable of taking care of anything he wanted done."

"Well, we're just having trouble getting the equipment to work."

"What kind of equipment? What is he working on?"

"I'm not really sure. He hasn't shared everything with me. He...um...he said something about not telling me anything before I needed to know. I'm pretty sure he's afraid I'll tell you everything and he doesn't trust you at all." He thought that would be a plausible excuse. He hoped she bought it. Hoped his delivery was believable. He studied her face, trying to read her reaction. Her eyebrow raised on one side as she seemed to stare directly into his skull. It seemed like an eternity till she spoke.

"I guess you're probably right. I can see where he might harbor a little distrust. See to it you work harder to gain his trust and be sure you report back sooner the next time. I'm sure he has something up his sleeve, something we can make a lot of money on."

"Oh, if I learn of something like that, you'll be the first to know!" He felt confident answering this way since McCoy wasn't intent on doing anything just for the profit. He still had a feeling she wasn't quite buying his whole story. It seemed like a good time for him to open the door and leave.

"Ted?"

The sound of her voice made him cringe and he hoped his disappointment in not making a rapid escape didn't show. "Yes, boss?"

"I expect your next report shortly. I see he trusts you enough to let you use his van, so the rest of the story should soon follow." Her voice seemed to be very foreboding at that moment.

"We'll see. I'll keep my eyes and ears open for new developments. You can count on me."

"Oh I will, Ted, I will." Her voice had taken an even scarier tone. "And if you cross me, I'll make sure it will never happen again. You could find yourself sliced up into little pieces. Scattered to the wind and no one would ever know you had even existed."

Ted just nodded silently and walked away. He always felt like he needed a shower after spending time with Ms. Wilson and he was pretty sure she could make good on her veiled threats if necessary. There was no time for any of that, though. He had to rush back to pick up Bradford and get to work on the next step of McCoy's plan. He sincerely hoped she didn't see through him and guess there was more going on than what he had reported on. He gave the receptionist a wave as he slipped out the doorway to the stairs to leave the building. He was even more anxious to get back to McCoy's after being with Ms. Wilson. He still felt a little strange about the feelings of darkness he was feeling around him, but the further he got away from the office, the less he thought about it. By the time he had the van back in motion and was waving to Tom the guard as he drove through the gate, those feelings of darkness were all gone. He couldn't tell if it was his imagination or not, but it definitely felt better as soon as he was off company property.

9
ARE YOU STARTING TO BELIEVE?

The morning rush hour was over now and there was barely any traffic on the road to Bradford's house. With all the strange feelings Ted had been experiencing, he had to wonder what Bradford would be feeling this morning. After all, he had not only been exposed to McCoy's influences like Ted had, he also got to spend time in a different person's body. Just the thought of it had Ted shaking his head. Everything was so very hard to believe as reality. He felt as if any second he would wake up and marvel at the strangeness of this incredible dream he'd been having. His train of thought was interrupted when he came to the street Bradford's house was on. McCoy had given him very specific instructions on how to get there, so it was easy to find the street. Ted wasn't prepared for the grandeur of the houses on the street, though. He knew Bradford was well-to-do, but he had no idea just how well off he was. When he came to the address on McCoy's instructions he found himself in front of a very large mansion surrounded by a tall brick wall. Ted parked the van in front of the massive wrought iron gates leading to the mansion and got out. As he walked around the van to the gates, he marveled at the intricate detail of the iron used in the gates. They must have cost more than Ted ever made in a year. He also wondered just how he was supposed to get through the gates to pick up Bradford. Almost as if they read his thoughts, the gates began to open.

"Hey, Ted!"

Ted was so engrossed in the enormity of the mansion and expense of the gates that he hadn't noticed Bradford had been walking towards the gate to greet him.

"Bradford! Let me guess, you're so excited to get to work today, you were waiting here for me to show up."

"Well, almost. I've barely slept at all after everything that went on last night. I'm not so much anxious as I am just caught up in this whole thing. I've been waiting here in my courtyard to see if you were going to show up or if this has all just been a bad dream."

"Well, buddy, I know where you're coming from on the dream thing. I'm sorry to inform you that if it's a dream, we're having the same one."

"I was afraid you'd say that."

"Let's get going. McCoy's probably waiting impatiently for us."

"You're probably right."

"Hey, don't you have to close your gate?"

"Don't worry, it's on a timer. It will be shutting itself here in about a minute."

Ted shook his head. "I should've known."

The pair got into the van and Ted turned it down the street to head for McCoy's house. He glanced at Bradford to try and read his attitude. This was an incredible experience they were both having and Bradford had made an even more incredible deal with McCoy than Ted had. Bradford seemed to be emotionless, so Ted had no clue what was going on inside his head.

"Still going through with it, Bradford?"

"Huh?"

"Are you still going through with it. You know, the deal?"

"Oh, that. I was really hoping that part was a dream."

"Having second thoughts?"

"No. Not really. McCoy helped me to see myself for who I am. It's an image I didn't like one bit when I really saw it. I actually kept playing it over and over in my mind last night. I'm hoping to change somehow by doing this. Going along with his deal."

"Buying into all of his spiritual talk, are you?"

"No. Not at all. I don't mind listening to him talk, but I'm not into that. You?"

"No, me either. It doesn't quite mesh with my scientific background."

"I can understand that. But McCoy's a top-notch scientist from what I've heard. How did that work for him?"

"Well, he tried to tell me about it, but I couldn't quite grasp how he got there. It is interesting to hear him talk though. Such an incredible mind the man has!"

"Can't argue that. I mean, look what we just went through."

"Yeah. I hope I can measure up to what he expects from me. Especially with the song and dance line I gave to Wilson."

"Oh, yeah. How did that go?"

"Scary. Very scary. Like looking into the face of the devil."

"There's that spiritual talk showing up. McCoy's changing you!" Bradford laughed.

"You know what I mean."

"I do, but don't you think it's ironic saying she's the devil right when we're talking about disbelief in spiritual things?"

Ted just looked at Bradford without replying. It suddenly struck him he had just compared the evil Ms.

Wilson to a spiritual being and he didn't believe in those. McCoy *was* getting to him.

"What's the matter, Ted? Wilson stuck in your head? You look like you just saw a ghost. And we both know there's no such thing."

"Yeah, that's it. A little Wilson goes a long way. A very long way."

"You know it. I hope she doesn't break you over this."

"Well, it can go one of two ways. If the pressure doesn't break me, she threatened to cut me into little pieces if she didn't get what she was after."

Bradford shook his head. "I've heard that one before. She's made the same threats to others after she's been doing drugs. They seem to amplify that evil personality of hers."

"Now you're the one talking about evil. McCoy would be proud of us both."

"I guess we'll soon see. We're at the house and I bet he's already waiting on me. Uh...us."

"Well it's not going to happen unless we're both here, so it won't be a party without us."

Ted put on the van's turn signal and pulled into McCoy's driveway. "Well, I guess that answers that question."

"What do you mean?"

Ted pointed to the garage door. "Look there. It started going up as soon as our tires hit the driveway. He's waiting on us."

Just like when they left, the door was completely open in perfect time for their arrival and began closing as soon as they were inside. After Ted put the van in park and shut off the engine, the pair both got out and silently approached the entrance to the elevator leading to the laboratory. Just like the garage door, it opened as they approached it. Although they exchanged glances, neither of them spoke a word. It was obvious to both of them McCoy was totally in control of the situation. It was no surprise to them to find him being the first thing they saw when the elevator doors opened.

"Gentlemen! Glad you decided to come back! I trust you're both well rested?"

"Well, I can't say I slept all that soundly or very much," said Bradford as he yawned loudly.

"Same here. A pretty fitful night," said Ted, also yawning in response to Bradford's yawn.

"I slept like a baby, myself. Not much, but it felt like enough. I had another vision and reprogrammed all the equipment for today's activity."

"What??" Ted couldn't believe what he was hearing. "But everything was working okay before, wasn't it?"

"In the vision I saw a better way of synchronizing the equipment. It will make your part of the job easier, Ted."

"But shouldn't we test it first?"

"I have complete confidence in the vision. I've also made notes to help you along the way. Oh, and in case something goes wrong, I have a complete outline of things you can try in every scenario I could think of."

"Doc, that doesn't give me a warm, fuzzy feeling inside." Bradford was obviously shaken by this new development.

"Don't worry, Bradford, I have great faith in my visions. And please, call me Carter."

"Well, Carter, this is a pretty intense thing you're asking me to do and now you're expecting me to rely on religious visions you get while you sleep?" Bradford was visibly upset.

"Now, now, Mr. Bradford, let's not get all excited. My visions are based on faith and relationship with the Creator, not 'religious' as you call it. I abhor religion myself."

Bradford had a stunned look on his face. He just couldn't grasp a religious person hating religion. Ted was also anxious to hear the explanation McCoy was going to come up with.

"Don't look so shocked Mr. Bradford, there's a big difference between religion and belief."

"I don't see the difference myself. I just can't see how you separate it into two different things."

"Therein lies the problem with most folks. They don't know there is a difference. Oh, don't get me wrong, organized religion has done some good things, but too many get caught up in their organizations with all the rules attached. They begin to serve their rules and their religion and forget about the almighty Creator of the universe and serving Him."

"And these visions of yours, you think they come from this...um...this Creator of yours? And you're serving this Creator by doing all this stuff here we're doing?"

"That's right."

"This definitely doesn't sound like any church I've ever heard of. I thought religious people only went to church on Sunday, sang a few old, tired songs, and took a quick nap during a boring sermon."

"That, my friend, is the religion I was talking about. Where there is religion, there is no relationship."

"Relationship?"

"Yes, relationship. It's one thing to believe in God. It's an altogether different thing to believe God."

Bradford was obviously puzzled. "I don't follow you."

"Take Ted and me, for instance. Before we met, I believed there was a Ted, but I didn't know him. I studied his exploits to learn more about him, but I still didn't know him. Then we met...started working together...now I can BELIEVE Ted because I know him, and he knows me. We have a working relationship now. It's much the same with God, Jesus, and the Holy Spirit. We can believe they exist, but unless you interact, work together, you'll never really get to know them all that well."

"Wow."

"That's all you can say? Wow?"

"This is just stuff I've never heard before. More than I

can process at this moment, especially with everything you have going on."

"I can certainly understand that. Before I got to know God, I would've said all of this is simply crazy. It's taken time, but I've learned to trust in Him and these visions He gives me. You can learn too, if you want to, although you may not get visions like I do. He may give you another special gift, an ability, to use for His purposes and glory."

"I think I'll pass for now. Maybe when I get older or something."

"Afraid to give control of your life to someone else? Want to do things your own way, do you?"

That was a question Bradford wasn't expecting. "Well...uh...well, yeah, I guess that's it. I don't want anyone telling me what to do."

"And yet you agreed to this grand experiment we're running here. You're already starting to change, but you won't admit it. God is already using you. Don't feel like you're alone, I confess to being headstrong and stubborn like yourself before I made my decision to follow Jesus. Part of the reason I chose Ted for this was his own stubbornness and penchant for doing things his way instead of being a corporate, ladder-climbing sheep."

Ted laughed out loud when he heard that description. "Baaa-aaa!"

McCoy found himself laughing too. "How about you, Ted? Are you starting to believe?"

It was a tough question for Ted. So much had happened, so many things were swirling around inside his head he didn't know what to believe anymore. McCoy made some interesting comments, yet all of his education didn't leave room for believing in spiritual things. Science simply wouldn't allow it. Yet, here was McCoy, the most scientific person he'd ever been around, talking about a god just like you would a regular person. All of this conflict inside coupled with the tension from Olivia Wilson was about all his brain could handle at once.

Pondering beliefs was just something that would have to wait for another time.

"I don't know, Carter. You make some good points. I'll have to think about it."

"You both will have to come to the knowledge on your own terms. I can't believe for you or make you believe. It's up to you as individuals. That's why I'm only sharing the beliefs I know with you and not trying to force you into anything."

"I respect that, Carter. I just hope I don't let you down. Wilson really tried to break me this morning. I hope I don't crack under all the pressure."

"Just stay strong, Ted. Stay strong and evil won't prevail."

"I'll do my best, sir." Ted couldn't help but notice the "evil" reference popping up again.

"Me too," added Bradford.

"I have faith in both of you and in the plan the great Creator has given me. It's time we get started. After we eat! I don't know about you fellows, but I'm famished!"

Ted and Bradford exchanged surprised glances. The events of the day had taken up so much of their attention, neither of them had given any thought to food or eating. They were equally surprised Dr. McCoy was the first to acknowledge hunger. But then, they should've known McCoy would think of everything.

"Over there in the corner I have a little table set up. Sandwiches in the mini-fridge next to it. Let's get to it so we have strength to get through the adventure of the day!" McCoy seemed so full of himself and cheery; a stark contrast against the sullen moods of Ted and Bradford. "Let's go, boys, the food's await'n!"

McCoy led the way to the table and started putting the sandwiches out for them. Ted and Bradford took seats around the table as McCoy started pushing sandwiches at them. The sight of food made them instantly famished and they both grabbed a sandwich and started pushing them into their mouths as fast as they could without being totally uncivilized. Both were well into their meal before they both simultaneously noticed McCoy hadn't yet started. He was there in silence, head bowed, offering what appeared to be a prayer before starting. He finished his prayer and looked up to see Ted and Bradford looking at him.

"What's the matter, you boys never see a man say grace before?"

"Well," said Bradford, "now that you mention it, no I haven't. Ted, how about you?"

"I...well...yeah, I guess I have, but it's been awhile. Not since I was a little kid. It's something I've never really given much thought to."

"Well you should."

"It's okay for some, I suppose."

"I can assure you, Ted, that God created all. Not some."

"I'm not sure I believe in any of that."

"You believe we all just magically appeared when a bunch of chemicals accidentally mixed in a primordial soup and turned into thousands of different species that just happen to work perfectly together in a common environment? That there's no intelligent design involved in the whole scheme of life?"

"I never really thought about it that much."

"You should. You're a scientist. You surely have run across more than one instance when your research gave you results totally opposite of what your professors in college professed to be irrefutable truth. That should make you question things."

"Well, yes. I have run into more than enough things that ran opposite of what I was taught."

"And you don't question the order of things?"

"I show up for work. Do as I'm told."

"Wilson has poisoned your mind."

"Wilson? She's a despicable, evil..."

"There! There it is! Ted you recognized the evil in Wilson!"

"So?"

"You've acknowledged the existence of evil. Surely you must understand the balance and recognize there is also good. God sent his son, Jesus, into the world to help protect us from evil. Then He left us the Holy Spirit for comfort and guidance!" McCoy seemed to be getting more excited with every word.

"You really believe this? All of this?"

"Think about it, Ted. Think of everything you and I have accomplished so far. How well things have gone? It's all because of the direction I've gotten from the Holy Spirit through my visions. We couldn't do this on our own. Certainly not in this short of a time frame."

Ted thought back to all he and McCoy had been through in such a short time. There always did seem to be some sort of magical way everything worked. Could it possibly be due to those things McCoy believed in?

"I can tell by looking at you Ted, the wheels are turning upstairs. You can ponder it a little longer while we eat. After that, I'll be needing your mind on what we're doing. I've added a few things to the equipment we'll have to go over before we start."

Ted nodded and went back to his sandwich. Bradford also started to eat again. He felt like a third wheel when it came to the interactions between Ted and McCoy. It was obvious to him those two had formed a bond between them beyond what either of them even realized.

Even though Ted and Bradford had a head start on the meal, McCoy was the first finished. The pair watched as McCoy wheeled over to the equipment and started pressing buttons and arranging cables. Bradford didn't comprehend much of what was going on, but Ted admired the care and attention to detail McCoy was displaying as he went about his tasks, whistling what Ted recognized as a hymn, as he worked. Ted soon finished his sandwich and joined McCoy by the equipment with Bradford following close behind.

"Carter, is it just me, or did you change a lot of the equipment around?"

"It was my latest vision from the Holy Spirit, Ted. The final purpose of what we're doing hasn't been revealed to me yet, but the changes are in preparation for it. I don't know what's coming, but I can already feel it's pretty important. Pretty important that you're a part of it, too."

"I don't think if there is such a thing as this 'Holy Spirit' you talked about, that it would want anything to do with me since I don't believe."

"I know you can't see it now, Ted, but I can see it. You're starting to feel the truth. You don't know it yet, but it's on the way. Keep looking for the truth, Ted. When you find it...you'll believe as I do. In the meantime, we have work to do. Read over these instructions I've made up and see if you have any questions."

Ted read through the instructions and was amazed at the detail McCoy went into. His part in this was going to be pretty easy. He could see a lot more equipment now that wasn't in the instructions and guessed it was for the upcoming things McCoy was going to be shown in those visions of his. Visions made no sense to him, yet the things he saw happen in this very laboratory, things McCoy said all came from these visions, made his head swim. He read through the instructions a second time to make sure he thoroughly understood it all, this time comparing the notes with the equipment.

"Ted, I see what you're doing and I like the way you're going about this. It makes me feel good knowing you're giving it your all to make sure it all goes right."

"I'm just following your orders here. You're the one who's making it all work."

"Me, you, and the Holy Spirit. Now the two of you help me out of this chair and get me on the table."

Ted and Bradford carefully lifted McCoy onto the table

as he instructed.

"Okay, now Bradford, you get up on the other table right there."

Bradford looked a little scared and uncertain, but he got up on the table as instructed.

"It's up to you now, Ted. The instructions tell you where and how to hook the equipment up to us. I know you'll do it perfectly."

"The way you have everything laid out and with these instructions you gave me, I don't see how I could possibly screw it up."

"Well, let's see that you don't, okay?" Bradford's voice was a little shaky as he spoke. The fear was starting to show.

"Don't you worry, my friend. We have the wisdom of Dr. McCoy behind us."

"In God we trust, Ted. In God we trust." McCoy's voice had a reverent, almost mystical tone to it.

"You do your trusting in God, and I'll be trusting your instructions. If there's a problem, I'll be blaming you, not God." Ted tried his best to project a happy voice to put everyone at ease. He could tell Bradford was having none of it, looking as scared as ever, while McCoy had an expression on his face so peaceful it freaked Ted out a little bit.

"There's still time for you to see the truth, Ted. Just keep your mind and heart open."

Ted nodded to McCoy as he began to follow the instructions and hook the equipment up to the two men, starting first with Bradford. With each electrical line, each connection, Ted began to see a pattern behind how McCoy had the transmissions back to the equipment arranged. The consoles themselves remained a mystery to him, but everything he was to look at during the transfer was clearly spelled out in McCoy's instructions. Ted was thankful for that because McCoy had changed everything around since the last time McCoy had everything fired up.

"You're doing good work, Ted. I knew you'd pick this up easily."

"It's not me. It's your equipment and your instructions. I'm just following along here. Most of the notes I took the last time don't apply since you changed a lot of the equipment already."

"Couldn't help it, Ted. I saw in my last vision changes needed made for our next project."

"Next project? What's that about?"

"I don't know, Ted. When I find out you'll be the first to know."

"You don't know?"

"The Holy Spirit hasn't seen fit to let me in on it just yet."

"You mean...you mean...you basically don't know where we're heading with this?"

"No."

Ted thought he noticed Bradford starting to quiver.

Ted shook his head. "But how..."

"I can't tell you how, Ted. What I can tell you is every step up to this point has been perfectly orchestrated from what I've received in the visions. Perfectly. I know you don't believe there is a God, Ted, but He believes in you. You've been a part of my visions and you surely can't argue the things we've done to this point couldn't be accomplished just through the wisdom of any scientist you've ever met."

That was a point Ted couldn't argue. He didn't believe in miracles, but everything he'd seen to this point seemed miraculous. It was definitely beyond his wildest imaginations.

"I'm sorry, sir. I shouldn't doubt you. I'll trust what you've done here."

"Like I said before Ted, in God we trust. In God."

Ted nodded this time and continued to finish the hook-ups on Bradford and then go to work on McCoy. McCoy's frail body was easier to attach the electrodes to, so that part of the job went easier. McCoy started humming a tune that sounded like some sort of hymn and that seemed to calm Bradford down. Ted couldn't help but notice the smiling, serene look on McCoy's face as he was attaching the electrodes to his body. It was almost as if his face was glowing.

"Okay, Carter. I think I have it all hooked up to your specifications. I've checked everything twice and it all seems in order."

"And from what I could see, it looks like you've got everything all ready and in perfect order. On to the next step of the adventure, Ted! Administer the injections from the hypodermics on that work station in front of you. Do mine first, because my vascular system will be moving slower than Bradford's."

Ted nodded and injected the substance into McCoy first, and then gave the substance to Bradford. Bradford's eyes darted back and forth a bit, but at least he seemed to be calming down a little better.

"Okay, Ted. Time for the next step. You know what to do." McCoy's calm voice was a comfort at this point for Bradford and Ted both.

Ted nodded to McCoy. This was the hard part. This was where he flipped the switch. This was where there would be no turning back. He slowly placed his hand on the control lever. Pausing a moment, he looked over at McCoy. McCoy's eyes caught his and he gave him a big smile and nod of approval. That was the extra push Ted needed to pull the lever.

The equipment immediately began displaying many lines of computer code on one screen while another displayed sine waves of activity from each man. A third screen, directly between the two men, had a split screen display, appearing to monitor other functions of the two men. Ted thought this one was capturing the movements of what McCoy believed to be the souls of the men. Lights and graphs on this monitor seemed to correspond with the colors of the wires going to the two men's bodies. The actions of the equipment were similar to the first time Ted had watched this process, but McCoy had changed so much already there was no way to be sure what was the same and what wasn't. One thing was very much the same, though. The sounds coming from the machines were musical in nature, just like the last time. The songs of the soul as McCoy called it. The sounds were different this time though. Ted listened for the depressing rhythm he had heard coming from Bradford before, but it was no longer there. Instead, the tones he assumed to be coming from Bradford were more neutral in nature, notes that seemed to just move back and forth without much change up or down. The sounds coming from McCoy were another thing altogether. The homeless man had an upbeat rhythm to his soul and Ted had expected something similar from McCoy. Instead, the sounds from McCoy were more like a magnificent orchestra playing out from just one instrument. Ted could hardly believe he was hearing such magnificent music from the console before him. Could McCoy actually be right? Could this magnificent music be coming from the soul of this magnificent man? Had Bradford's music changed because his soul was actually changing? Ted immediately put that thought out of his mind and concentrated harder on the equipment in front of him. Science simply wouldn't let him start to believe in souls like McCoy did. It couldn't be possible. Or could it? There was an intense battle going on inside of Ted over these beliefs and he had to put it all aside so he could monitor the activity going on before him on the screens.

Just as it happened with the homeless man, Ted could see two different colored lines approaching each other on the screen between the two men. The instructions said the next lever on the console had to be pulled when those two lines intersected. As they got close to one another, a sound much like a smoke alarm began to blare out from the console in synchronized fashion with the screen that was now flashing. Just as the two lines intersected, the screen changed colors and the alarm sound became constant. That was Ted's cue to pull the lever and he was ready to pull it at the exact instant the equipment told him to. As soon as the lever was pulled, all the noises and flashing lights stopped. The lines on the monitor steadily went in the opposite directions they had before. Ted felt just like a railroad engineer who had just flipped the switch to change tracks for a big locomotive. He let out a sigh of relief now that the important part of the procedure was behind him. McCoy really had things set up to go smoothly and Ted was really thankful for that. According to the instructions, all he had to do now was wait for the transfer to be complete and turn off the equipment. This gave him time to study the faces of the two men as they lie there before him. He couldn't do that with the homeless man because he and Bradford were both sedated for that transfer. This time, both men were conscious for the procedure. Ted looked intently as the serene expression started to fade from McCoy's face. It was blank for a few moments and then began to take on the fearful, anxious expression that Bradford had been wearing. Ted was a little apprehensive, but he had a feeling he'd know what he'd find when he turned to look at the expression on Bradford's face. Sure enough, Bradford was now wearing the peaceful, serene look of McCoy on his face. Ted was numb. Even though he'd seen this procedure before, it was still so very hard to believe. Everything McCoy laid out worked perfectly. Ted really didn't believe all this soul stuff McCoy talked about, but how could he be so right about everything going on with this equipment, the visions giving him perfect direction in everything, and then be wrong about the soul? Ted was really having trouble getting his own non-beliefs to measure up with all this hard evidence happening in front of him. So many things were spinning through his mind right now. A beeping noise coming from the console woke Ted up from his swirling storm of thoughts and signaled the transfer was complete. Ted looked at his watch. It seemed like this thing had gone on all night, when in reality, it had only taken about 15 minutes. It was time to flip the levers back and disconnect the equipment.

10
IT WORKED PERFECTLY

Ted felt really strange and nervous waiting for whatever would happen next as he began disconnecting the electrodes from the men. What if none of this actually worked? What if the procedure somehow damaged both men? Ted had visions of trying to explain to the authorities how he ended up with two mindless zombies, how it would all play out in the supermarket tabloids, and how he'd be spending a long, long time in prison.

"Daydreaming again, Ted?"

"Bradford! You're okay!"

"Yes, Ted, I am. But I'm over here."

Ted did a double-take. He should've been prepared for this, but it was still a shock to him when Bradford replied from McCoy's body.

"It worked again, Ted! Did you have doubts?" Now he realized McCoy was talking to him from Bradford's body.

"I've had doubts all along the way. But I had faith in your abilities. I have to admit, it's still a big shock to hear you guys communicating from each other's bodies."

"It wasn't so much my abilities, but the guidance from

above. That's where the faith should be."

Ted was momentarily frozen in time. He wasn't really sure what to do next, but that didn't stop McCoy from starting to disconnect himself. Now that he was in Bradford's body, McCoy had no trouble taking care of that simple task. As soon as he was done with his own connections, he hopped up off the table and began working on Bradford, who was now residing in the body once inhabited by McCoy. It did feel very strange, that sensation of looking down at himself while he was disconnecting the electrodes, but it wasn't nearly as strange as the feeling he had by being in Bradford's younger body. He suddenly felt like a kid again, so young and vital! Bradford was still getting acclimated to being in an old, feeble body. Every time he tried to move something, it didn't work like it should. He could only make his arms move and they felt so weak he wasn't sure they were moving or it was his imagination. It reminded him very much of the feeling when McCoy had him drugged for the first transfer.

"Ted, give me a hand getting Bradford into my wheelchair. He'll probably have a little trouble adjusting to my body."

McCoy's words snapped Ted out of his momentary trance. "So, how are you both doing? Everyone feeling okay?"

"I'm doing great," answered McCoy, "how about you, Bradford?"

"I feel like you drugged me again. So weak, and I can barely move anything."

"Sorry about that. My old body doesn't work so well these days. Yours, on the other hand, is wonderful! I feel so alive!"

"I hope it suits your purpose. And I hope it suits that purpose as fast as possible. I'm not sure I can get used to this worn out body of yours."

"Don't worry, my friend. I've gotten the impression

from my visions time is of the essence. We won't have any time to waste if I'm interpreting things properly."

Ted shot McCoy an irritated look as he helped pick Bradford off the table. "You mean there's a chance you're off the mark with this whole fiasco?"

"Don't worry, Ted, we're on the right course. I may be foggy on a turn or two, but we're heading in the right direction. The Holy Spirit will fill in the blanks right when we need to know the details. For now, there is much work to do."

The pair eased Bradford into McCoy's wheelchair. It was a little awkward for him to get into a comfortable position, but McCoy knew just how to place the body into the chair having occupied it himself for so many years.

"There you go, Bradford," McCoy said, his voice sounding gentle, like a parent, "You'll find the chair to be reasonably comfortable after you get used to it. I've dismantled most of the controls which work many of the automated functions around here, so you needn't worry about hitting the wrong button. If you need anything, just ask. I have everything available in this house to easily tend to that old body of mine."

"Well, that's comforting to know. Doc, this is a big risk I'm taking. A really big risk. If something happened and I'd end up stuck in your body, I don't know what I'd do. I really hope it all works out as you planned. It better work!"

"It will. Thanks to the guidance of the Holy Spirit through my visions, I have all the faith in the world it will work. And thanks to you and Ted for joining in on this. No matter how obedient I am, it wouldn't matter if the two of you hadn't also joined in. Ted, I can see from the expression on your face you have a bit of turmoil going on inside you. Don't hold it in, let me know what's on your mind and if I can't help, I can aim you in the direction of someone who can."

"Thanks, but no thanks, Carter. I'll figure this out myself." Ted's voice couldn't hide his uncertainty over everything going on.

"I had a feeling you'd say that, Ted. It's important you figure this out on your own anyway. I am here to help if you need it, though."

Ted was still having a little trouble mentally grasping McCoy's words coming from Bradford's mouth with Bradford's voice, yet it was unmistakably McCoy behind them.

"Thanks, Carter. I appreciate it. But let's move along here. What comes next?"

"Next? Next, I have a lot of work to do before we continue, Ted. I have to make some more modifications to the equipment and construct some new pieces to add in. I won't be needing you for a bit, so you can have some time to yourself. I'll let you know when I need you, or you can just hang around here if you want. Bradford, here, has fewer options and is pretty much stuck watching me work."

"Hear that, buddy? You're a captive audience."

"I hadn't thought of it that way before, but you're right," replied Bradford. I'm totally committed now, so it is what it is. No turning back now."

"No turning back for any of us," replied McCoy. "The wheels are in motion."

"Yeah. Wheels." Ted still seemed to be deep in thought. "You know, I think I'm going to go out and wander around a bit if you don't need me here for anything."

"Go on, Ted. You've earned a break. I've got a lot of work to do before I get another vision and find out the next step in our journey, whatever it may be."

"I wish you wouldn't put it that way. It makes me feel like we're walking blind."

"We are walking blind in a manner of speaking, Ted. God is leading us one step at a time."

"Yeah, sure." Ted felt something stirring deep down inside him each time McCoy mentioned God or that Holy

Spirit thing. He usually thought the feeling was an annoyance, but now he wasn't sure anymore. He wasn't sure of much of anything with all the things he'd been seeing and going through lately.

"Take care, Ted. I'd wave, but I don't think I'm capable."

Ted looked over at Bradford and could see his arm feebly raise up a little. "I will, buddy. Watch over the doc, here, till I get back. I know you'll be taking good care of Bradford, Carter, because you're actually taking care of yourself." Ted chuckled at his own little joke.

McCoy laughed in return. "Get out of here, Ted. You're holding real progress up!" McCoy winked at Ted to let him know he wasn't serious.

Ted shook his head and waved his hand in the air as he turned and walked away from them towards the elevator. He turned and looked out into the room as he got in and saw McCoy was already working feverishly at a new piece of equipment and Bradford was intently watching him work. It struck Ted as an odd scene, yet it was a scene he belonged to. That strange feeling inside him was rising up again as the doors closed.

11
IN NEED OF A RESCUE

Ted mindlessly drove his car away from McCoy's house. There was something gnawing at his insides and he didn't even know what it was. He was sure McCoy would say it was his soul. At the start of the day, Ted would've argued that point, but now, after the day's events, he was beginning to question all the things he thought was reality. His mind kept replaying the moment when McCoy answered him from Bradford's body. It just didn't seem real, but there it was in front of him. He couldn't help thinking that maybe McCoy was right. Maybe everyone did have a soul in them. But that would go against everything he had ever been taught. Yet, he couldn't help thinking what he had witnessed gave more evidence to the existence of a spirit inside than any theory he heard or presentation he watched. This was real. At least he thought it was real. Maybe he was going insane and these things weren't even happening. All these thoughts were bouncing around so much Ted didn't even realize his mindless driving led him back to the hillside overlooking the homeless settlement. Just like that first time McCoy took him there, Ted turned off his engine and looked down on the settlement below him. They seemed to be simple people, just intent on living and staying warm, not much more. Ted could see the homeless man they "borrowed" down below, just sitting peacefully by his campfire, keeping warm. There was something about the simple scene that appealed to Ted. Nothing in his life gave him the simple peace this man seemed to have. Before McCoy called on him, his life was nothing but disappointment and depression. This man seemed to be far more content with just his small fire. Ted got out of his car and walked down the hillside towards the man. Even though he was a stranger, the man didn't seem to be afraid or apprehensive as Ted approached.

"Hey there, old-timer!" Ted tried to be as unassuming as he could, so as not to frighten the man. The man answered, but his voice was low, the words mumbled. Not being able to understand him, Ted continued.

"Mind if I sit here by your fire a moment?" The man motioned for Ted to sit.

As Ted sat by the fire, he began to look around and notice some of the others nearby in the settlement. They seemed to be so different, yet so similar. They all seemed to be content with their simple lifestyle, but he could tell the circumstances bringing them to this place were probably very different. Some seemed to be burned out from some sort of substance abuse, some seemed to be down on their luck bringing them to this end. A few of the others seemed to be living this lifestyle by choice, actually enjoying this simple off-the-grid existence. Ted studied the face of the homeless man beside him. There seemed to be a complex story behind his eyes Ted couldn't read. Now and then he mumbled a word or two in Ted's direction, most of which Ted couldn't understand. This simple man, who seemed to have nothing more than the clothes on his back and the fire before him even offered Ted something to eat at one point. That act of kindness began to make

Ted so emotional, he knew he had to get up and leave or risk breaking down and crying in the presence of this man. Thanking the man, Ted got up and started to walk around the settlement. He still didn't have any sort of clear direction as to what he was going to do with himself until McCoy called for him, so he decided to get a good look at the entire encampment before leaving. He was admiring the handiwork of a thrown together shelter at the opposite end of the encampment when he heard the sound of several cars approaching. Within seconds, three expensive-looking cars where sliding to a halt within several yards of where Ted was standing. Several young people rapidly got out of each car and started walking in his direction. A chill came over him as he recognized some of them as the same gang who McCoy told him terrorized these people.

"Look guys, this loser's a little more well-dressed than the rest of the rabble. Must be a new arrival."

"Let's make him the first to leave!"

"Yeah, let's send him merrily on his way!"

"Yeah, let's get him!"

Ted kept turning around, looking for a quick exit, but the gang had him surrounded in no time. There was no escape. They were armed with pipes, chains, and ball bats. Obviously none of them were there to discuss the weather, politics, or religion. He was starting to wonder if maybe he should be saying a prayer or something. McCoy always said he should have a relationship with the Creator. It looked to him right now like the gang wanted to send him to meet the Creator in person. One of them awkwardly swung a bat at his head, but he saw it coming in enough time to duck the blow. There was no way he would be able to dodge another.

"Help me." The whispered words instinctively left Ted's lips. They weren't loud enough for anyone else to hear, so quiet Ted wasn't even sure he said them, but he did. The thought flashed across his mind that maybe those two simple words were his first prayer. The thought also crossed his mind that it might be the last prayer he ever uttered. The one who appeared to be the leader of the group began laughing maniacally and started taking warm up swings to prepare for contact with his intended target. Ted raised his arms, ready to make some defensive moves, when he heard it. The deep, roaring sound of a large motorcycle was heading their way, and it seemed like it was coming at a high rate of speed. The gang all heard it the same time as Ted. They all turned towards the sound just in time to see the large motorcycle show up, circle the group, and slide to a halt in a cloud of dust. All eyes were on the massive rider of the bike as he methodically set the kickstand and climbed off the bike in a slow, deliberate manner. This was definitely the same man McCoy had talked about and they had seen before.

"Evening, folks. Here we are again. Nice night to be alive, eh?" The big man seemed to be in a cordial mood.

The leader of the group barked out some orders to the others. "He's only one man! We can take him!"

The leader and two others approached the big man, spreading out so the leader directly faced him and the others came from either side. Ted watched as the leader rushed the big man, bat swinging directly at him. It all happened in such a flash Ted could hardly believe his eyes. The big man dodged the head-on attack while grabbing the pipe out of the hands of the attacker on his right at the same time. As soon as the pipe left his hands, that attacker turned and ran for his car. The leader drew back to take another swing, but the big man used the pipe to knock the bat from his hands. Having seen this, the attacker to the left made his move. The big man caught his bat in mid swing, causing the attacker to lose his footing. The leader lunged at the big man while this was going on, but got knocked aside with such force he went rolling away, almost the whole way back to where Ted was still standing. The second attacker got up off the ground and just stared at the big man. His eyes grew as the big man effortlessly tossed the pipe back and forth from hand to hand. The attacker dropped his bat, raised his hands in surrender, and slowly started backing away towards his car. Ted was close enough to hear the leader muttering obscenities under his breath as he slowly got up. He appeared to still have plenty of fight left and approached the big man once again. Ted was amazed at the calmness the big man displayed. He didn't even appear to be preparing to fight, just standing there with his arms lowered as the gang leader paced around him, looking for the perfect opening to attack.

"You know you could just turn and leave," said the big man in a calm, non-threatening voice.

Ted watched in disbelief at the scene before him. The gang leader started to laugh like a crazy person and charged right at the big man, furiously swinging his bat at him. The big man looked like he was just going to stand there and allow himself to be hit, until at the very last second, he ducked out of the way and spun around behind the gang leader and swatted him to the ground with a sharp blow to his back. Before he could get up, the big man stomped down on the hand holding the bat, causing the gang leader to scream in pain. The big man reached down, threw the bat aside and lifted the gang leader up off the ground and held him at eye level, his feet dangling off the ground below him.

"So tell me, young man, just what did you have in mind for our friend over there? I'm sure it wasn't anything bad, now, was it?"

"Uh..uh..." The gang leader was obviously feeling very scared without his bat to protect him.

"Really, you didn't intend any harm, now did you?" Even under these circumstances, the big man seemed happy and was smiling.

"N-n-n-no...uh...of course not. We were just playing around." Ted thought the gang leader was on the verge of crying.

"Well now, that's nice of you. Only one problem.

Might you know what that is?"

"Uh...uh.....n-n-no, sir."

"Well, I'll just tell you then young man. The problem is I don't believe you. I think you meant to harm our friend here. Isn't that what you really meant to say?" The big man started to shake the gang leader a little bit while he was asking the question.

The gang leader's face looked pained as he replied. "Yes. Yes. I meant to hurt him."

"Now that's more like it. Jesus told us not to lie. He also told us to treat people like we wanted them to treat us. Now, I'm sure you didn't want our friend over there to go after you with a baseball bat now did you?"

"Uh...no."

"I didn't think so. Good thing I showed up in time so you didn't make the mistake of mistreating our friend here. Wouldn't want you to do that and go against Jesus, now would we?"

"Jesus is just for those wussy church people." It shocked Ted to see the gang leader suddenly show some defiance. It would prove to be a mistake.

"What did you say?" The big man snarled out the words as he pulled the gang leader close to his face. "I hope you weren't insulting my Jesus, young man, or we will have words." The big man's demeanor had changed and even Ted felt scared of him at that instant. He could see fear reenter the gang leader's face too.

"I mean...uh...uh...well...Jesus is just a made up person, uh...uh...right?"

The big man snarled. "He's every bit as real as you are. And if you're not careful, you might get to meet Him real soon."

Ted feared the big man was about to lose his temper and do some real harm to the gang leader. He must have been having the same feelings as he began to cry.

"No, please. Please. Please don't hurt me. Please don't."

The big man's expression instantly softened and he let the gang leader down, although he didn't let go of him.

"I'm not going to hurt you. Jesus is real. Jesus loves you and died for your sins. Mine too. I suggest you go and find out as much about Him as you can. If you'll agree to do that, I'll let you go, okay?"

The gang leader was crying so hard, all he could do was nod in agreement. As promised, the big man let go of him. Ted thought he might run away, but instead, he crumpled to the ground in a crying heap, probably weak from the ordeal. The big man kneeled next to him and placed a hand on his shoulder. It looked to Ted like he was saying a prayer. It was a very short prayer and the big man got right up and walked over to Ted.

"You okay, young man?"

"Yes. Yes I am, thanks to you."

"No need to thank me, I'm just doing as I'm told. All the glory goes to God."

"Huh?"

"God told me to come here tonight."

"Well, whatever, I'm thankful." Ted stuck out his hand. "My name's Ted."

The big man's hand engulfed Ted's as he began to shake it. "My name's Jim, Jim Dunning. Some of my friends just call me Big Jim, but it doesn't really matter what you call me. Pleased to meet you, Ted. Just what brings you here tonight anyway? I can see by the way you're dressed, you don't belong here."

"I was just out wandering, thinking things over, and ended up here."

"Were you happening to be thinking about spiritual things?"

"Well, yes. But I'm not a spiritual person by any means."

"Maybe you should be. I believe it was the Holy Spirit that brought you here tonight."

Ted shook his head and looked down at the ground.

"That's something he would've probably said. I just can't get away from McCoy's influence."

"McCoy? After McCoy?"

"Yes. Dr. Carter McCoy."

"This really was the work of the Holy Spirit then. I met Carter not too awful long ago. He's my brother in the Lord and a good friend."

"I thought that might be the case. He mentioned you to me once. Something about protecting these people here."

At that moment their conversation was interrupted by the sound of the gang leader's car starting up. While they were distracted with their conversation, he had sneaked back to his car and was escaping.

"I guess he wasn't enjoying hanging out with us." Jim said, laughing as the car sped off into the night.

"Can't say as I blame him, the way you took care of him like that."

"I'd prefer not to, but it seems to be the only method guys like that understand."

"So you really do protect these people!"

"I can't take the credit for that. Usually, I'm just minding my own business and God tells me to come over here."

"What? God tells you?"

"Yeah. It's almost like I can hear His voice sometimes."

"So you're hearing voices, and McCoy's getting visions. And it all seems to work." Ted shook his head, obviously confused.

"Not a believer, I take it?"

"Well I...I wasn't...but what's been going on these last few days...and just now. I don't know. I just don't know."

"The Holy Spirit told me there'd be someone here seeking answers, seeking Him."

"You mean..."

"Yeah. I was sent here to protect you tonight. And He

told me to hurry."

"You'll have to excuse me, but my head is really spinning here."

Jim laughed. "Been there, done that. I totally understand. I was there once myself."

"How did you figure it all out, get your answers?"

"A good friend of mine helped me. He could probably help you too, if you like. Want to go see him?"

"I don't want to impose on anyone. Especially at this time of night."

Jim laughed again and slapped Ted on the back, nearly knocking him over. "Brother, if you knew what I've put that poor guy through, you know this would be a little thing for him. I'm pretty sure he'd be upset if you didn't show up with me tonight."

Ted was torn. He didn't want to bother anybody with what he had going on within himself, but yet, there seemed to be a hole inside, something missing he couldn't put his finger on, something that just wouldn't go away. He remembered how McCoy had said this mountain of a man was a fascinating individual. Maybe it would be best to go along with him and see where McCoy's fascination came from.

"Okay. You win. Where's this friend of yours?"

"He's over the mountain in the next town. You can ride behind me on my bike, but I'm afraid I don't have a helmet for you."

"That's quite alright. My car is parked over there." Ted pointed up to where he parked his car above the homeless settlement.

"Great! You go hop in your car and follow me. We'll be there in no time."

"Will do. Just lead the way."

12
MEETING MAX CARSON

Ted was mentally numb as he turned the key to start his car. He wasn't sure what he was feeling at the moment. He was going to follow the big man back to talk to his friend, but he wasn't even really sure why. It wasn't so much he wasn't feeling anything. That nagging empty feeling he had inside was something he couldn't understand; something that wasn't going away. Maybe he was just looking for answers as the big man said. Maybe this friend of his had the answers. Maybe he would know how to make this empty feeling go away. A small animal running across the road broke Ted's train of thought and brought him back to full attention. Just how long had he been following that motorcycle in front of him? They had long since left the city limits and had been traveling through a forest for some time, even though Ted hadn't really paid attention to it. He had been daydreaming so much, going over things in his mind, he didn't even know where they were or how they got there. All he could do was trust this big man, this Big Jim Dunning person, knew where they were going, because he sure didn't know. Just as Ted thought he would be lost forever in the wilderness, the tree lines started to fade away and it appeared they were approaching a small village. Sure enough, there was a town sign along the road beginning to appear in Ted's headlights up ahead. He made sure to go slow enough as he drove past it so he could read whatever the sign had to say. "Welcome to Brooksville" was all the sign had to say, but that was enough. Now Ted had an idea of where they were. He'd heard of the small town before, just a drive over a mountain and through a state forest from the city where he lived, but he'd never been there. From what he'd heard, there was really no reason for anyone to go there unless it was where they lived. It was mostly dark under the night sky, not being lit up like daytime under security lights like it was where he came from, so Ted couldn't tell very much about what the town was like. He could make out the shape of a church steeple up ahead and it appeared to be where Mr. Dunning was leading him. It was also one of the few buildings they were passing having a light on, which struck Ted as odd in comparison to the rest of the town. It almost felt as if their arrival was expected. Sure enough, just as Ted had thought, the big man aimed his motorcycle towards a small parking lot by the side door of the church where it appeared the light was coming from and parked. Ted pulled in beside him and turned his car off and got out.

"So, this must be the place."

"Yep, this is Brooksville Community Church. The friend I was telling you about is the Pastor here."

"Looks like your friend keeps rather odd hours."

"Well, if I know Max, he's in there because God told him to be because we were coming."

"Wait, God told him that we were...uh, Max, did you say? Max Carson?"

"Yep, my buddy Max Carson. You don't already know him, do you?"

"No. No I don't. It's just I should've known. McCoy

told me about him and I should've connected the dots."

Jim laughed. "Ol' Carter sure covered all the bases. That man is amazing! God really gifted him for sure!"

"Yeah, in the short time I've known him, he's definitely proven to be a unique individual."

Jim laughed. "Unique. Good way of putting it. I think you'll find Max unique too."

Ted just shrugged. He really had no expectations of what he'd find when they went inside. Along with the empty feeling inside, he was also starting to feel like he was supposed to be on this little adventure tonight, like he belonged in this very spot at this very time. It was all such a very strange feeling to him, not like anything he'd ever experienced before. Whatever was behind this door the big man was leading him to, he was starting to feel sure it was his destiny. A destiny he would soon meet as the big man threw open the door.

"Max!" The big man immediately called to the man inside, rapidly walking over to him and giving him a big handshake and hug, a display of brotherly affection Ted had never witnessed in the city.

"Jim! I should've known you'd be behind this! God told me to be here and I've been busy praying for whoever or whatever He called to be here for tonight."

"Max, this is my new friend Ted. I found him over in Tallinn at the homeless settlement. I brought him here because I think he's looking for answers. And I think you'll be able to help him."

Max laughed and winked at Jim. "So you 'found' him, eh?"

Max stuck out his hand to welcome Ted. "Any friend of Jim's is a friend of mine. Welcome!"

Ted shook Max's hand. "Pleased to meet you, Max. I've actually heard about you, from my friend, Carter McCoy."

Max's eyes lit up. "You know Carter? He's an incredible man. I've always felt God put a special calling on him from the first day we met!"

"Well, there's something on him alright. I don't know what it is, but it's something."

"The way you say that I'm feeling you're not a believer. Ted, God's put it on my heart that you're feeling an emptiness inside. An emptiness because you have a God-sized hole in your heart that needs filled."

Max's words stopped Ted cold. How could Max know he was feeling such emptiness? This 'Holy Spirit' thing these guys kept talking about was baffling to him, yet Carter, Jim, and Max all seemed to talk about it like it was reality. A reality that gave them secret information, which quite frankly, scared him a little bit.

"Well, yes, I guess you could say that."

"I'm sensing you have some inner turmoil in you. An internal struggle."

Ted paused to think about that before answering. "Yes. Yes I do have a struggle. So much has happened recently, so much that goes against what I've learned, what I've been taught, it's starting to leave me confused, to be honest with you."

"Are you starting to feel different inside? Like something's leading you?"

Ted was really getting uncomfortable with how accurate a man who had only known him for five minutes was getting with secret things going on inside him.

"I can tell you're getting uncomfortable, Ted. I'm not a magician or wizard, these are just things the Holy Spirit is telling me. Am I off the mark?"

"No. No, you're right on the money. I don't understand how you know these things, but you're saying exactly what I've been going through."

"Ted, you're looking for answers. It's a search for God, that's what's going on. A search to know Him. I can't find Him for you, though. You'll have to come to your own understanding. Carter went through the same thing. You're probably a bit like him. So very much knowledge, so much education and training that goes against the existence of a god, yet you come to a point where there can be no other explanation for how this physical world works."

"How do you know all this stuff about me?" Ted was starting to get a little unnerved with all this.

"Well," Max replied casually, as he pointed skyward with his right index finger, "He knows and lets me in on it."

Jim chimed in, "It's just how it works when you get to know Him. The Word says His sheep know his voice. We follow Jesus, so we're His sheep. I won't lie to you, Ted, I thought this stuff was pretty weird too, until Max taught me how to seek after Jesus. I was a 'see it and believe it' kind of guy. Then I learned from Max you have to believe it before you see it."

"I don't think I could ever get to where I believe like you guys do, the things you believe in."

"Jim didn't think so either, did you, buddy?"

"Ted, if you had met me awhile back...well, I'm not the same man as I was then."

"Amen to that!" Max laughed loudly.

Jim gave Max a playful punch on the shoulder. "You didn't have to agree so easily, buddy!"

Max rubbed his shoulder a little. Even though the punch was playful and in jest, Jim was so strong it still stung a little bit. His mood became more solemn as he turned towards Ted.

"Ted, I can tell all of this is a lot for a man of science like yourself to swallow. Carter and I had some long talks when he was working out how his scientific knowledge was colliding with scriptural wisdom. He is far more intelligent than anyone I've ever met before, and he finally concluded science actually meshed with scripture instead of contradicting it. I wish I could go into more detail, but his scientific knowledge is way, way more than I can comprehend. When he started to have visions, visions he told me were far above his understanding, I knew he was connected into the Holy Spirit."

"You know about his visions? He hasn't given me many details, but they've definitely led him on a course I don't understand. Things make no sense to me, yet fall into place perfectly. He even told me the reason he chose me to help him was because of those visions."

"If that's what he told you, that means the Holy Spirit is using you, too. Do you feel it? Do you feel something guiding you, something you can't quite put your finger on?"

"Well...now that you mention it, everything that's been going on has seemed like a strange path. Like my steps are taking me places I don't want to go, but everything works out somehow."

Jim nodded his head. "Yep. I remember what that's like. When you accept it, give yourself over to Jesus, and follow those steps freely, it'll really blow your mind."

"You talk a lot about Jesus. I remember stories about Him from when I was little. Those stories are more like fairy tales, aren't they?"

Ted cringed a little. His words had made Jim straighten up and bristle a little. There was definitely a fire in his eyes now. "Nope. Jesus is real. He's as real as you and I sitting here. And not only that, He died on a cross so we could live forever with Him."

"Easy, Jim," Max said softly as he placed a hand on Jim's shoulder, "our friend here is just not acquainted with the Lord yet. You can relax, Ted. Jim tends to get a little excited when people try to tell him Jesus isn't real."

"Yes, Jim, please forgive me, I didn't mean any harm." Ted was more than a little frightened, especially when he saw the tattoos on Jim's biceps rippling a bit when he was talking.

Jim's face and tone softened. "That's alright, Ted. Like Max said, I get a little sensitive when people talk about Jesus. I thought it was all a fable once myself, but now He's more than real to me and the best friend I have."

"I don't understand. How can Jesus be your friend?"

"I talk to Him all the time. And through the Holy Spirit, He talks to me, too."

Ted didn't know what to say. Between all that was going on at the lab and all this spiritual talk, his brain was overloaded. Max could tell he needed a break.

"Ted, I think you have a lot to think over. Jesus loves you and wants you to know Him better, but I don't think you're quite ready to give up your own world just yet."

Max walked over to a nearby table and picked up a book off of it and brought it back to Ted.

"Ted, here's a copy of the New Testament I want you to have. It's written in an easy to understand modern language. If you read it and ask the Holy Spirit for guidance, I believe you'll get to know Jesus better and hopefully make a decision to accept Him as your savior. Here's my card, please call me if I can help or you can just show up here if you want. Jim will help you too, but he's a little harder to get a hold of. I think we've given you enough to go on for one sitting."

Ted felt emotion creeping in. Emotion that hadn't been a part of his life since he was a child. He tried to stop it, but the tears started to flow down his cheeks and he couldn't do a thing about it.

"I'm...I'm...sorry. I don't mean to be this way. I don't understand why I'm feeling like this."

Max smiled as he spoke. "It's because you're changing, Ted. The Lord told us in the book of Ezekiel, 'I will give you a brand new heart and put a new spirit in you; I will remove your heart of stone and give you a heart of flesh.' That's what's going on inside you, Ted. That heart of flesh is beginning to grow."

Ted nodded. He wasn't sure if he believed what Max was saying or not, but he couldn't deny it. Something was indeed changing inside him.

"Thank you. Thank you both for everything. You've given me a lot to think about. Quite frankly my head is really spinning."

"No doubt, my friend, no doubt," said Jim sympathetically, "I remember exactly what it's like. Can I pray for you before you leave? I'll keep it short."

"Yeah, sure."

Jim placed a hand on Ted's shoulder. Ted could feel the power in that huge hand and was thankful Jim was on his side.

"Father, Jesus, please protect my new friend, Ted, and lead him down the right path so he'll get to know you like we do. In your name, amen."

Ted was shocked the prayer was so short, simple, and heartfelt. All the religious prayers he'd heard before in his life were so long-winded and meaningless. He was really beginning to think these guys really knew what they were talking about.

"Ted, do you want me to lead you back to where you came from?"

"Thanks, Jim, but I think I can make it on my own."

"Well, you just be careful of deer jumping in front of you when you go over the mountain. They should really be moving around right about now. And say hello to Carter for me when you get back."

"I will, Jim, and thanks again for everything. Thanks to you and Max both."

Max nodded. "Remember, we're here for you if you need anything. And Jesus is with you wherever you are, just ask Him for help if you need it."

Ted nodded, shook both their hands, and left.

"What do you think, Max?" asked Jim as the door closed behind Ted.

"There's a lot on that young man's shoulders, Jim. We need to pray for him."

"Amen, brother. There's a spiritual battle going on all around him. Let's pray now."

The two men knelt in prayer at the altar in the church as they heard Ted's car slowly leaving the parking lot.

13
A VISIT FROM THE DRAGON LADY

Ted awoke with a start and sat straight up in bed. When he got home, he only meant to take a quick nap, but he could tell he had been asleep much longer than he intended to be. He knew it was around 3 a.m. when he got home, but the brightness of the sun in his room suggested it was more than just a couple hours that had passed. His alarm clock was of no help. The flashing "12:00" told him the power had been off, and of course, he had never gotten around to getting that backup battery replaced. Carter had promised to call if he was needed, so his phone obviously had not made any noises to wake him. Now just where had he left that phone? It wasn't on the nightstand. Not in his pockets. It wasn't on the counter beside his car keys. Thinking it may have fallen from his pocket on the way in from the car the night before, he went out, retracing his steps between the car and his house. Still no phone. He was starting to feel some anxiety, wondering if McCoy had called and he wasn't there to answer.

"I'd better get something to eat, make a sandwich, so I can keep my energy levels up. Then I'll head over to

McCoy's and see if he needs me," Ted thought to himself. He had to laugh at himself when he opened his refrigerator door and found his phone inside. "Wonder where my head was when that happened?" he said out loud to no one in particular. There were no missed call notifications, so McCoy had not tried to reach him. The clock on his phone also told him it was late afternoon. He had slept almost 10 hours! Little wonder considering how mentally draining the activities of the last day were, what with the transferring of McCoy into Bradford's body followed up by the attack on him at the homeless settlement and the late night visit with the big man and his pastor. And what a visit it was! Ted still couldn't quite get his mind wrapped around this idea of Jesus being real. It just made no sense. What bothered him the most, though, was now all the truths he believed in before were now beginning to make even less sense. He was thinking through those things while eating his sandwich when he noticed the Bible the pastor gave him the night before on the table there beside him.

"Couldn't hurt to take a look inside, I guess," he thought to himself.

Not having any knowledge of the Bible, he just randomly opened the book up to see what was inside. At the top of the page, it said "Acts 17" but that didn't mean a thing to him. He figured it would be best if he just started reading at the top of the page. "Starting from scratch, he made the entire human race and made the earth hospitable, with plenty of time and space for living so we could seek after God, and not just grope around in the dark but actually find him. He doesn't play hide-and-seek with us. He's not remote; he's near. We live and move in him, can't get away from him!"

Ted felt like he had been struck by lightning. This was what the pastor had been saying. He'd have to find God on his own. And now this book was telling him to not only look for God, but that God was near and not hiding from him. It was as if God was trying to tell him something through the words of this book in front of him.

"Easy, Ted, ol' boy," he thought to himself, "you're starting to think like those other people."

Ted's thoughts were interrupted by a loud knock at the door. He peeked through the window to see who was there and was shocked to see Olivia Wilson, in the flesh, standing on his doorstep. He had no doubt his blood pressure was starting to rise in response. Ted had only paused a second, but she still began to pound on the door much harder, obviously impatient. It was against Ted's better judgment, but he opened the door anyway.

"Good day, Ms. Wilson, what brings you here?"

"You should know quite well why I'm here, Crosby."

Ted started to feel a presence of evil around him, like there was a darkness invading his space. "Not really, why don't you enlighten me?"

"McCoy's made a breakthrough and you didn't report to me!" The words practically hissed from her lips like a snake and were followed by several obscenities.

Ted felt a cold chill falling over him. "Breakthrough? News to me." He tried to play it cool, but for some reason, he was starting to feel terrified inside.

"You can't hide things from me, I'll find out. I always find out. You'll be sorry if you try to hide anything! McCoy has to be up to something. My sources say they've seen Tony Bradford over there. Tell me why McCoy would have him there! Tell me NOW!"

Ted could have no trouble imagining her face contort into that of a demon, in fact, at the moment he was having trouble not visualizing it as demonic. It was baffling to him as to why he would think such a thing. A few days ago, he wouldn't have, but after listening to McCoy talk about it then spending time with Jim Dunning and his pastor, these thoughts were suddenly finding their way into his head.

"ANSWER ME!"

The shrieking voice brought him out of his thoughts.

"I don't know."

"Why you…" Wilson launched into a stream of obscenities. Ted was thankful she didn't have a gun. The sound of her verbal assault on him definitely gave him the impression she was capable of killing at that moment.

"I guess Bradford was just in the right time at the right place for them to become friends."

Wilson poked her finger into Ted's chest sharply. "Listen, you. I know Bradford. He's not 'friend' material for someone like McCoy. Something else is going on there."

"Maybe. But if there is, I don't know about it." Ted was only stretching the truth a little. There was definitely something going on, but he hadn't been let in on the secret yet. The way he was being grilled, he was glad he didn't know more. It felt as if Wilson's eyes were burning right into him, trying to burn out his very heart and soul. He began shaking his head at the realization he was now thinking of having a soul. Lucky for him, the head shaking fit into his excuse for Wilson and didn't raise any more questions or suspicions.

"Find out, Crosby. Find out or there will be consequences. I don't think you want consequences, now do you, Crosby?"

He could only imagine what she meant by 'consequences' but the way she was acting, he surely didn't want to find out. "I'll find out what I can."

"See that you do."

"Yes, sir. I mean, ma'am." Ted intentionally called her 'sir' out of spite. He didn't think it mattered, because he was getting the feeling she enjoyed intimidating people into doing things like that by accident.

"Watch your step, Crosby. You just watch your step." Wilson made a threatening gesture to Ted as she turned to walk away.

Ted let out a big sigh of relief as he closed the door and leaned against it, looking to the ceiling. Maybe there was something to this spiritual stuff after all. He had doubts before, but now there was no way anyone could convince him the evil he was feeling when Ms. Wilson around wasn't real. He was so focused on that evil feeling he jumped straight up when the ring tone of his phone went off unexpectedly.

"Yo, Ted, is that you?" The voice was unmistakably McCoy's but the words and tone were equally unmistakable as being Bradford's.

"Yeah, buddy, what's up? McCoy need me to come over now?"

"No. He's so wrapped up in something he told me to call you and tell you to stay put till tomorrow morning. Something about wanting to make sure no one got in his way while he's on a roll. I gotta say I'm really amazed at how hard he's working. I had no idea I was capable of moving so fast." Bradford laughed at his own joke.

"Yeah, that McCoy is amazing. I probably would just get in the way, but I wish I could watch."

"I bet. So what's up, Ted? What's going on? I'm picking up a little distress in your voice."

"Oh, you can tell? Our friend, Ms. Wilson, just left."

"Ah, the original witchy woman. I guess that explains that. Pretty hard on you, was she?"

"The only way I can explain it is...is...evil."

"Let me guess. Glazed eyes. Pupils slightly dilated. Extremely hostile? Showing signs of anxiety?"

"Well, yeah, that was pretty much her."

"Sounds like she's had another evening or so of her favorite recreational drug with friends."

"You think?"

"Yes, I saw it many a time from being in the same party circuit. You're probably lucky she wasn't armed."

"Funny you should say that. I had the same thought while she was here."

"Doesn't surprise me a bit. You didn't tell her anything about what's going on did you?"

"How can I? I don't know what's going on. Do you?"

"Well, I can't say that I do. I've been watching McCoy work all day and don't know any more than I did before. I can tell you he's building another contraption. I'd like to tell you more about it, but my technical knowledge pretty much ends with a screwdriver."

"Don't sweat it, it's pretty obvious you weren't brought into this whole thing to use screwdrivers."

"I have to tell you, this is actually pretty creepy. I mean, sitting here nearly helpless while I watch myself working so hard and so fast on things I don't even understand."

"I can't comprehend it myself. Everything I've seen, everything I've watched...words escape me."

"Hey, gotta go. McCoy's calling me over to hold a wire in place. See you tomorrow, okay?"

"Yeah. Sure thing. Give my regards to McCoy."

"Will do. Later!"

Ted was secretly happy he had a chance for another night's sleep. He wouldn't admit it to anyone else, but his body was aching and he was drained emotionally from Wilson's visit. The extra time would definitely help him to get fully recharged. He could only guess what he was getting recharged for, but Wilson's hostility made him all the more determined not to let McCoy down.

14
A TROUBLING VISION

Ted was awake at the crack of dawn on this day. It hadn't been the best night's sleep, but he still felt more refreshed and stronger than he did the day before. There were a few bad dreams of being tortured by Ms. Wilson, but he had still managed to get some good sleep. He was also full of the anticipation of learning what today would hold in store at McCoy's place. After all the amazing things he had seen and been a part of to this point, he could only imagine what this new equipment McCoy was building would do. The anticipation kept growing with each passing moment as he was getting ready to go. For McCoy to be so intensely working on this, it had to be something magnificent. Ted was so consumed thinking about what McCoy was cooking up, he had already mindlessly driven several miles towards McCoy's place without realizing it. Ted couldn't help but begin wondering if McCoy's visions were actually some sort of divine revelation. The things that had been happening were nothing short of miraculous. Miraculous. A word Ted wouldn't have even thought a few days ago, let alone use. And now, he was entertaining the thought there might actually be such a thing as a miracle. Or was there? As he pulled into the driveway at McCoy's house, he could see the door automatically opening to greet him. Some would think it a miracle, but he knew it was McCoy's technical wizardry making it happen. The only thing keeping him from giving McCoy credit for all the "soul" stuff was the fact McCoy took none of the credit himself. Always said it came from his "visions." Maybe it did. Maybe it was real. Ted was really starting to have trouble with reality these days. He knew this door he was walking through was real and that was about it.

"It's about time you got here!" Bradford's voice was shaking and he sounded scared. Coming from McCoy's old, worn out voice box, it sounded even worse.

"What's going on?"

Bradford pointed over to the corner of the room. It was darkened, but he could make out the outline of Bradford's body in the corner. It was at that moment he noticed the sobbing noises coming from that corner.

"What's wrong with him?" Ted's worry showed in his voice.

"I don't know, man. I found him like this when I woke up this morning. All he's been doing is blubbering and babbling incoherently. I've been hoping you could get through to him."

Ted's emotions were running a hundred miles per hour as he walked over and knelt beside McCoy.

"Carter. Carter. It's me, Ted."

"Oh, Ted. Ted. If you could see it. If you could feel it." McCoy started sobbing uncontrollably again.

"What is it, Carter? Did you have one of your visions? What is it?"

McCoy looked at Ted and nodded slowly. He started to take deep breaths and try to get himself under control so he could speak.

"I...I heard...I heard them, Ted. I heard them." McCoy

started sobbing again.

Ted took him by the shoulders and looked him in the eye. "Heard who, Carter, heard who?"

With the saddest eyes Ted had ever seen, McCoy answered. "I heard them, Ted. The unborn who were murdered. I heard them all, Ted. All of them at once."

Ted let go of him and looked at McCoy with a look of shock and disbelief. "Murdered?"

"Yes, Ted, murdered. All murdered by abortion."

"And you heard them?"

"Yes. In my vision. God revealed to me what He hears. He hears the screams of them all. And when I awoke, the feeling was still so intense, I could actually feel the fluttering of an unborn child about to be aborted within me like it was real. So very real. I could swear I could even see it move."

Ted was floored. It took him a few moments before he was able to speak.

"I don't get it. How does this fit into what we're doing here? Are you sure this vision of yours isn't your imagination this time?

Those words broke McCoy out of his funk. "Imagination? How dare you say such a thing? This is real! A revelation from God himself!"

The anger behind McCoy's words took Ted by surprise and actually scared him a little. It didn't help that McCoy's words were more imposing coming from Bradford's younger body and not his old, decrepit one.

"Easy, Carter, easy. I just want a little more explanation, okay? You have to admit this is totally different than what you've shown me so far. Just let me in on the secret, okay? Let me in on what's going on."

McCoy studied Ted's face and thought about what he had just said. The expression on his face softened.

"You're right, Ted. I apologize. I was being much too harsh."

"I apologize, too, Carter. You've got way more going

on than I could ever handle. I should try and understand that better."

"Ted. I know now. I know what we're to do. I did some research on the internet and confirmed it. It's unbelievable."

Ted laughed. "As if anything we've done to this point has been believable. What is it?"

"Have you watched the news on TV lately? Seen anything on the Terri Sullivan story?"

"Yeah, I think so. Isn't she supposed to be brain dead and kept alive artificially? The state's won the right to remove the feeding tube and let her die?"

"That's the story. My vision showed me it's not the reality."

"Say what!!????"

"I looked it up this morning and my vision was backed up by some obscure news reports. The news media's burying the reality. Terri Sullivan was a pro-life activist. During a protest at an abortion clinic years ago, she was bludgeoned by a pro-choice activist and suffered spinal and head injuries the media say left her paralyzed, in a coma, and in a vegetative state."

"Yes...and...?"

"The whole purpose of what we've been doing here in the lab, the whole thing, has been about her."

"The whole thing? What? How is any of this going to keep them from letting her starve, and why's it so important to keep her alive when she's a vegetable anyway?"

"That's the point. My vision has shown me she's not in a vegetative state. All this equipment, everything I've put together here...is to fix her. The vision showed me how."

"You're kidding me. That's insane. Absolutely insane."

"And there's more."

"More?"

"More. Remember our homeless friend?"

"Yeah. How could I ever forget?"

"Turns out he has a name. Captain Terrance Sullivan. He's Terri's father."

"No! That's incredible!'"

"Seems he lost everything and became homeless trying to get justice for his daughter."

"Wow. There's no way to top this story."

"Well actually, there is."

Ted's mouth dropped open. "Surely not."

"There's just one more detail that puts the cherry on the top of it all. We need to save Terri...because in the future, one of the unborn children she ends up saving...will find the cure for cancer and other diseases."

Ted couldn't speak as he was processing all this new information. He was overwhelmed by the enormity of it all. McCoy could sense Ted was having a mental overload, but there was still one more piece of information he had to know.

"And Ted...there's one more thing you need to know."

Ted was shaking his head. "How...just how...how could there be any more?"

"It's about our timeline. Our time is short."

"Short? Short how?"

"My equipment has shown me my body is weakening. There isn't much time left before I have to get Bradford back in his body. We have to be done before we reach that time. My time in this world is short."

15
I SORT OF KNOW THE PLAN

"I don't want to die." Bradford was visibly shaken.

"I know it probably feels like an empty promise to you, but I'm going to make sure that doesn't happen." McCoy was doing his best to sound reassuring, but he wasn't sure Bradford was buying it.

"That's easy for you to say. If something goes wrong, you've got a perfectly good body to live in. I'm trapped in your dying body." A tear slowly rolled down Bradford's face.

McCoy placed his hand on Bradford's shoulder. "I can assure you that won't happen. My equipment precisely monitors what's going on in that body. I'll know when it becomes too much of a risk to go on. And here's another thing you can put your trust in. I'm not afraid to meet my Creator face-to-face. I look forward to it. Unlike most people around here, when my time comes, I'm ready to go. I'm not going to miss that train."

Bradford still had a noticeable sadness in his eyes. It was hard for McCoy to see him like this, even harder still since he was actually looking into his own eyes. Ted was listening to the whole conversation, helplessly watching, and feeling a sadness knowing he was going to lose one of his two friends no matter the outcome.

"Carter, are you sure of this? Sure there's no other way?" Ted tried to sound like he wasn't pleading, but he was.

"No Ted, this is our destiny. No one lasts forever. The important thing to focus on here is we have an important job to do. We must save Terri Sullivan. We must save her so she can return to being the voice of the unborn. So she can save the baby who will grow up to cure cancer and potentially save millions! There's a lot riding on this, Ted. A lot!"

Ted hung his head, his eyes fixed on the floor. "Yeah. I know. I just...it's...Carter, I just don't want to lose you yet."

McCoy looked at Ted and smiled. "Ted, I have no one in this world. You've been the closest thing I've had to real family. We haven't known each other long, but I feel we've formed a very unlikely friendship, a true bond. I am ready to go home to meet my maker, but you've made these last weeks some of the best of my entire life. I wish I could stick around longer, but my time is nearly up. Let's just treasure what's left."

Bradford spoke up. "Hey, it's been nice getting to know both you guys, but I'm not ready to...as you say..."go home" or anything like that. I've done bad things. I deserve to be stuck in this body for a time, maybe even deserve to die in it, but I don't want to. I'm not ready for that. You two had better get your act together and see to it I get back into my own body before it's too late, okay?"

Ted and McCoy both looked at Bradford. It was obvious to the two of them he was terrified. And little wonder, he was a young man trapped in a failing old man's body. A body he had just learned had little time left.

"Bradford," McCoy spoke softly, "this thing can't happen without your contribution. You have my word we'll be successful. With your body, I'm getting so much more work done in such a short time. Using your body is an absolute necessity for me, just as my visions have shown. We've come too far to turn back now. This is God's plan. You must trust me and believe it."

"I'm trying to trust you, McCoy. It's just that I'm so scared."

"I understand. Trust in God and He will give you peace."

"I don't think I can do that. But you're here and real, so I'll try to put my trust in you. Everything you've said has worked so far. I'll trust you." Bradford's voice was still very shaky.

"Okay, Bradford, you can do that. But when this is over, just remember, I was only following God's plan. All the glory for this plan will go to Him when it's done, not me."

Ted caught something in McCoy's words and spoke up. "I heard you say 'plan.' Am I to understand you have a plan in mind? You already know what comes next?"

"Well," McCoy replied a little sheepishly, "I sort of know the plan."

"Um...sort of? I'm not getting a warm, fuzzy feeling from 'sort of.'"

"Well Ted, I know the 'whats' and 'whos,' I just don't know all the 'hows' that will be involved."

"I guess that's a start. So just 'what' are we going to do?"

"We're breaking Terri Sullivan out of the rest home where they have her."

"You're kidding me. Tell me you're kidding me."

"It's no joke, Ted. No joke at all. That's where the vision was murky for me, though. I don't really know how it's going to be done, but I do know I need to call a friend of mine for help."

Ted's eyes lit up. "I bet I know who."

McCoy looked doubtful. "Really, Ted, I doubt you know."

"I think I've got you on this one, Carter. You're going to call your good friend, Pastor Maxwell Carson."

"What!!??? How did you figure that one out? Did you have the vision too?"

"No. I had the pleasure of meeting your friend the other evening. And I'm suspecting a part of this breaking out plan will involve the muscle power of his rather large friend."

"So you met Dunning, too? How did this happen?"

"Long story. Let's just say he showed up to help me out of a jam and leave it at that."

"A story involving Dunning's help certainly has to be one worth telling."

"We have to get to work on this plan. Place the call and I'll tell you the story later."

"Good idea, Ted. We really have no time to waste. I'll call Pastor Carson now."

16
WE NEED HELP

"Hello?" Pastor Carson had been sitting by the phone. He didn't know why, but had a feeling he'd get the answer as soon as the phone rang.

"Max? It's Carter. How are you doing?"

"I'm fine Carter. But your voice, there's something very different about your voice. Are you okay?"

"I'm fine, I'm fine. You're right, my voice is different, and it's very hard to explain why right now. But don't worry, all is well."

"That's good to hear. Carter, I'm feeling something in the Spirit, is it another of your visions? Is that why you called?"

"Well, yes, yes it is. We need help."

"We being?"

"Me. Me and my friend Ted."

"Ah, Ted. We just met the other night. A good man. Now tell me, Carter, what do you guys need?"

"We need your help to...uh...to...uh...um, break into a nursing home."

Max was quiet for a bit before he spoke again. "Did I

hear you right, Carter?"

McCoy laughed. "Yeah. I'm afraid you did. Pretty wild, eh? Breaking into a nursing home?"

"Wild wasn't quite the term I had in mind, but we'll go with that. Should I ask why, or am I better off not knowing?"

"Well, now that I think of it, if we get caught by the authorities, it's probably best you know as little as possible."

"Understood. And just what's the name of this place I know nothing about?"

"Sacred Haven of Rest."

"I know the place. I'll tell Jim. It's probably best I stay out of it in case something goes wrong and I have to help bail you out of it afterward."

"Good idea. And thanks, I feel a lot better knowing the big guy will be there to have our back. There's an employee parking lot out behind the main building. The back row borders a forest and it's not well lit. Have him meet us there tonight after the sun goes down. Give me a call as soon as possible if that won't work for him. We're on a tight schedule here."

"Will do. Be careful, Carter. I'll be saying some extra prayers for you all."

"Thanks, Max. I have a feeling we'll be needing it. Talk to you later."

Ted seemed energized from listening to McCoy's conversation. "Did I hear right? Dunning's going to be helping us?"

"Pastor Carson said he'd tell him about it."

"That's awesome! Since I've already seen what he's capable of, I feel a whole lot better about this breaking in thing."

"Agreed. I'm sure glad he's on our side."

Bradford seemed a little puzzled. "He's just one guy. How can you two be so enthused about just one guy?"

"If you saw this 'one guy' in action, you'd know," Ted

replied.

"I don't know if you're familiar with the story, Ted, but Dunning does seem to be a modern day Sampson. I think he could knock down the door by himself if he had to." There was definite admiration in McCoy's voice.

"Well it certainly helps calm me down a little knowing my fate is being helped along by a guy like that," said Bradford. "I'm still scared though."

"Well you just sit there and be scared while Ted and I load some medical equipment into the van. Lord willing, we'll be transporting a very important patient tonight."

Bradford showed some anxiety in his reply. "Well that Lord of yours had better be willing, because I don't want to be the next one transported around here...in a hearse!"

"Easy, Bradford," replied McCoy, "you'd better conserve whatever strength that old body of mine has left."

"Hey, forgive me for being scared, but I have reason to be, okay?"

"I can't argue that. Pastor Carson taught me that it helps to read Psalm 91. It's about God's protection and not being afraid. Whenever I feel fear creeping in, I read the words there and it always helps me. You can use that computer built into the chair to bring up the words and read them. Trust me, if you read and believe, it will help. Meanwhile, Ted and I have some work to do."

"I'll read it, but I can't promise the 'believe' part."

"Fair enough. Keep your mind open. And your eyes, too, because God's going to show up here in a mighty way, you'll see!"

"He better!"

McCoy just smiled warmly at Bradford as he and Ted left to begin loading the van for the plan. Ted was amazed at the medical equipment McCoy had at his disposal. When they stepped into the storage room, it felt like walking into a hospital room.

"Carter, why do you have all this stuff?"

"Research, Ted, research. If it weren't for the profit Wilson and her cronies thought they could milk out of my research, hardly any of this would be here."

"Good ol' Wilson. Where would we be without her?"

"I don't know about us, but there would be many more happy people around if she were somewhere else."

"Do you really think she's a bad person, Carter?"

"I pray for her, Ted. But she's following a path that will only lead to destruction. She may climb high on the corporate ladder, but it will do nothing for the state of her soul. I feel sorry for her."

"Wait a minute. You feel sorry for her?"

"Yes, Ted, I do. She's wasted her life on her own pride and never really got to live. It's a very sad state of existence. Leaves one very empty inside."

Ted thought about McCoy's words as they loaded all the equipment into the van. He, himself, knew of the empty feeling. It was the same empty feeling that gnawed at his very being so many days as he sat at his desk at work. He still had it, yet something seemed different, as if he was changing inside. He had been thinking it was all due to McCoy's influence, but he was starting to have doubts. Seeing so many things his mind could only reconcile as unbelievable, listening to McCoy quoting scriptures and giving all the credit to God, well...Ted was starting to think maybe there was something to all these spiritual things McCoy talked about after all. In the short time since he'd gotten close to McCoy, Ted's whole world had changed and he was no longer sure of anything.

"Ted?" McCoy's words brought Ted back from his thoughts.

"Yeah, Carter?"

"That was the last of it. We're ready to go. You looked like you were in deep thought. Anything in particular?"

"No, nothing particular. Just rehashing current events."

"God is good, isn't he?"

"Whatever you say, Carter, whatever you say."

McCoy smiled to himself. He could see a change happening in Ted, a change he hoped would keep growing in his soul.

"Let's go, Ted. We should be there at about the right time to meet our friend, Jim."

The garage door smoothly opened as always as the fully loaded van pulled out and, as always, closed perfectly after them.

"So what's the next step of the plan when we get there?"

"I don't know," replied McCoy, casually.

Ted nearly swerved off the road. "What do you mean you don't know!!??"

"Just what I said. I don't know."

"All this attention to detail, our every move being guided every step by your visions...and you don't know what we're doing next."

"No. I'm assuming you and our friends will have to take care of it. It wasn't covered in my vision, so I think I don't have much to do with it."

Ted rolled his eyes. "Great. Just great. Nothing like going into something crazy like this blind. How can you be so calm at a time like this?"

"God's got it under control. Our friend, Mr. Dunning, is a man of God. He'll be led by the Spirit. It won't be a problem."

"If it were anyone other than him, I'd really be concerned. I think he could probably do it all by himself if he wanted."

"I have great confidence in him as well, but he'll still need me for the medical assistance. And I'm sure you'll be contributing, whatever your part in this will turn out to be."

"You're not helping."

McCoy laughed. "It'll be alright, Ted. It'll be alright."

"But how can you be so sure?"

"God will let us know what to do when we need to do

it and probably not a moment sooner. It's one of the things I had a great deal of trouble dealing with myself. I always wanted to control as much as I could myself. Giving everything over to God and letting him run everything...well...I just believe it's the hardest thing for any of us to do. If you read the Bible, you'll find even the disciples, the ones who walked with Jesus and witnessed His miracles first-hand, had trouble doing this. I can't lie to you Ted, I still have trouble with it, but I am much better at it than I was before and I work at getting better at it every day. I hope one day you will too, Ted."

"We'll see. How about we just get through this day first, okay?"

"Fair enough, Ted, fair enough. Looks like we're here already. Time sure flies when you're having fun with friends, eh Ted?" McCoy let out a little chuckle.

"I certainly hope this little adventure flies by without us landing in jail." Ted didn't sound very hopeful.

McCoy chuckled again. "Trust in the Lord, Ted, trust in the Lord. There, right there, it's the alley leading to the parking spot behind the building where we'll be meeting our friend." McCoy pointed to an unassuming alley beside what Ted recognized as the main building of the Sacred Haven of Rest. There were only a couple lights out behind the building and Ted could see the back row where they were to meet Dunning had no light reaching it. It would be practically impossible to see anything back there from the door after dark.

"That's the spot. Right back there, Ted."

"I can see you've chosen well. We'll be as invisible as ninjas back there."

"I don't quite get your reference, but yes, we'll be well concealed in the dark. Under that tree looks like a good spot."

"Alrighty, then. That's where we'll park."

"Keep your eyes peeled for Dunning. He could be arriving any minute as well."

"There's an ugly, antique truck heading our way. Think it could be him?"

"Yes, I've seen that truck. It's him. Ted, you have to get out and do the talking. He's not aware I'm in Bradford's body. Try to explain it so he's not too shocked when he sees me."

"Wow. I didn't think of that one. I've gotten used to it, but I remember how much of a shock it was to me at first. And I knew something was happening, even though at the time I didn't know what."

"Exactly. Try to break it to him gently. Time is of the essence, though, so try to get to it quickly."

"Yeah. Sure. No pressure, right?"

"Don't worry, Ted. You can do it!"

Ted got out of the van and waited for the truck to park. Sure enough, Dunning was the driver and he got out to meet Ted. What Ted wasn't prepared for was the two other people that got out of the truck on the other side.

"Ted, my man! Good to see you again!"

Ted stuck his hand out for a handshake. "Good to see you again, too, Jim."

"Ted, I want you to meet my son, Joshua, and his friend, Sheila."

Ted exchanged handshakes with the two of them. "Pleased to meet you both. Jim, I thought you'd be the only one meeting us tonight."

"Ted, I'm not sure if you understand it, but I had a feeling in my spirit that Joshua should join us. Oddly enough, he had a feeling Sheila should come along. That's why the three of us are here. So anyway, where's Carter? I thought he was to be here with you."

"Well, Jim, uh...I'm not sure how to explain this to you, so I'll just come right out with it. Carter's here in the van, but you won't recognize him."

A look of concern came over Jim's face. "What's happened to him? Was there an accident? Can I do something for him?"

Ted was touched by the big guy's immediate shift to deep caring. It wasn't something you'd normally expect from someone who looked so mean. "No Jim, nothing like that. Nothing like that at all."

"Well what is it then?"

"He's in a different body."

Jim said nothing. The two young people who were with him exchanged puzzled glances. Ted knew he should probably say something, but he didn't know what. The silence became very uncomfortable.

Finally Jim spoke. "Okay, Ted. If you say it, I believe it. We were all called to be here for a specific reason. There's no rule saying it all has to go like we expect it to. What do you think, Joshua?"

"I think you're absolutely right," said Joshua with an almost defiant tone, "we're here to do spiritual battle, so earthly rules need not apply. Sheila?"

"I'm with you guys. Ready to get to it!" Sheila's voice had the same defiant tone as Joshua's.

Ted stood there shaking his head. "That was way easier than I imagined. Before this happened, if I had heard the same thing I just told you guys, I know I would've just gotten back in the car and left."

Jim placed a hand on Ted's shoulder. "Don't beat yourself up over admitting that. We've all been there ourselves. Faith comes to each of us in different ways. You'll get there."

Ted nodded at the big man. He didn't know whether he was too scared or ashamed that he didn't share the faith these people did, but whatever it was, there was no way he was going to tell them his faith at the moment was in the abilities of McCoy. Ted turned and motioned for McCoy to join them.

"Good job, Ted! Do they understand what's going on?"

"They know you're not in your own body. I'm not sure if they understand any more than that."

"We'll catch up anything left hanging as we go, won't we Ted? Good to see you again, Joshua, how are you doing? And who's this young lady? I don't believe I know her."

"Um...I'm doing fine. This is my friend, Sheila. She's here to help out too. Is that really you in there Dr. McCoy? All the words seem to be yours, but the voice is totally different."

"Yes, son, it's me. Pleased to meet you Miss Sheila, it's a pleasure you could join us. I must say, you seem to be very calm under these strange circumstances."

"It's a pleasure to meet you, too, Dr. McCoy. Joshua and Jim have told me a little about you. The circumstances are a bit strange, but nothing has been normal for me ever since I met Joshua." Sheila smiled at Joshua as she replied to McCoy.

"Well, I think we all know each other now. Tell us, Carter, why are we here?" asked Jim.

"We're here to kidnap Terri Sullivan."

There was silence as Jim, Joshua, and Sheila all exchanged glances. Joshua finally broke the silence. "Isn't Terri Sullivan the pro-life activist who ended up in a coma years ago? The one they're about to let die?"

"Better tell them the specifics, Carter," said Ted.

"Specifics? Oh, yeah. That may help. I had a vision showing me how to fix Miss Sullivan's body and bring her back to life."

More silence followed McCoy's statement.

Sheila spoke up. "To sum this up, we're kidnapping Sullivan...and you're going to fix her, right?"

"That's right," replied Carter, "you're taking this right in stride. That's admirable."

"Buddy, if you knew some of the things I've seen while hanging around this guy," Sheila said as she pointed to Joshua, "you'd understand."

Joshua smiled sheepishly at Sheila, "yes, the Lord has led us on some pretty incredible adventures. If He could see us through those, he'll surely see us through this."

"You guys never did tell me about those adventures, but I like how you're thinking. God brought us here, and God will be with us on this adventure. Tell us what to do, Carter!" Jim replied excitedly, obviously getting ready to get started.

"Okay, Carter," said Ted, "the whole gang's ready to go. What's the plan?"

"Well, Ted, like I told you earlier, my vision didn't show me that part. Maybe that's why He sent three people to help us instead of just one."

"So what do we do?"

Jim spoke up. "They might have some sort of security cameras to identify us. Will that be a problem?"

"Well," answered McCoy, "even though our friend Pastor Carson couldn't, and shouldn't, be here with us tonight, he did give me a little bit of good information about this place. Since he comes to visit residents here on occasion, he knows the 'lay of the land' so to speak. Here in the back, there is only one security camera and it is over the back door there so it can record who comes and who goes."

"So how are we going to go in and get out without it catching us?" asked Joshua.

"Ted, get that small cardboard box out of the back of the van for me, will you?"

Ted nodded and went to the back of the van. He remembered loading the box up with the rest of the equipment, but had no idea what the box contained. He did have confidence in McCoy, so he had a pretty good idea whatever was in this box was sure to be very useful. His confidence in McCoy only got stronger as he saw the gleam in McCoy's eyes when he handed him the box.

"Here's the answer to your question, Joshua."

Everyone gathered around McCoy to watch what he was about to unfold.

"Is that what I think it is?" asked Jim.

"Yes, Jim. It's a drone."

"How's that supposed to help us?"

"Just watch," said McCoy obviously proud of what he had planned.

McCoy took the drone out of the box and set it on the ground. He next took out a small control console, one that had been obviously modified. Everyone silently watched as the drone took off and flew toward the rear door. McCoy watched intently on a tiny screen on the control console as the object of the flight came into view. At the exact moment his target was on the screen, he pressed a blue button on his controls. Everyone watched from a distance as it appeared a cloud of some sort shot out of the drone.

"Is that..." Before Ted was finished with his question, McCoy answered.

"Yes, I armed the drone with a paint canister. The lens of the security camera should now be a nice, plain shade of black."

Jim started to laugh. "I'm glad you're on our side, Carter!"

"Okay, guys, let's get to this," said Ted as he started towards the door and motioned the others to follow. All of them felt a confidence sweeping over them as they walked.

"What do we do now, Carter?" asked Ted. "We'll need an electronic key card to get this door open."

"Or a little inside help, eh?" Carter winked at Ted.

At that moment, the door opened and a slender man stepped out.

"Clete Diehl, I presume?" asked McCoy.

"Yep, that's me. Pastor Carson told me I might want to keep an eye out for you guys."

Ted shook his head. "Let me guess. You know Pastor Carson?"

"Yep. I can't go to church much because of when I work and I'm always on call when I don't, but Pastor Carson has a Saturday morning Bible study set up that works with my schedule. I try not to miss a single week."

"That Bible study is where I met Clete, Ted," replied Carter. "I told Max we might need a little inside help. He must've figured Clete was our man."

"But how did you know he would be here to let us in?" asked Ted.

"I didn't know, Ted. God is guiding our steps. I just trusted him."

Jim spoke up, "Guys, we don't have time for a sermon or fellowship. We have to be moving along here."

"Right you are, Jim! Clete, can you lead us to our target?" asked McCoy.

"Yes! Follow me."

The group followed Clete inside. He quietly led them down a hallway until they came to a doorway on the right of the hall. Clete put a finger to his lips to make sure they would all be quiet and led them inside the room.

"Folks, don't take this the wrong way, but you all stick out here like a sore thumb. This is the room where we launder the scrubs worn by the staff. Take a quick look through them and borrow something that fits you so you'll all blend in."

"Excellent, Clete!" exclaimed McCoy in a whispered voice. "Your idea will help protect us!"

"The Lord of all will be protecting you, not me." Clete winked at McCoy.

McCoy chuckled as he and the others sought out scrubs that would fit them. They all quickly changed into borrowed scrubs, looking to find the right clothing to fit them as Clete stood watch out in the hallway. Sheila changed behind a curtain and called out to the others when she found scrubs that fit her.

"Are you guys decent out there yet?" she called out in a hoarse whisper.

"I think we're as decent as we'll ever be," replied Joshua. "Come on out."

Sheila came out from behind the curtain and looked at the group all dressed in their newly-borrowed scrubs.

"How do we look, Miss Sheila?" asked McCoy.

"Well, pretty good for the most part, but..."

"But what?"

"Well, Jim, well, you know..."

Everyone turned to look at Jim. He was a comical sight to behold. A giant of a man in scrubs whose seams were begging for mercy.

"Uh..Jim?"

"Yeah, I know, Carter. But it's the best I could do. I'll try to be as inconspicuous as I possible."

Joshua laughed. "Good one! You! Inconspicuous!"

McCoy spoke. "It will have to do, Jim. We don't have time to get a tailor in here to custom-fit your outfit, so we'll have to go with what we got. Everybody else ready?"

Everyone in the room exchanged glances and nodded.

McCoy went to the door. "Clete? We're ready."

Clete stepped into the room to join them. "I have to get back to where I belong or my bosses will get suspicious. Here's what you'll have to do. When you leave this room, go right to the end of the hall. Then turn left and go to the administrative desk. Once you're there, look for the blue footprints on the floor. Follow the footprints to Room 189."

McCoy shook Clete's hand. "Clete, you've been a huge help. May God bless you."

"He does, sir, He does. And may He be with you and grant you success in what you're doing."

"I believe He will, Clete, I believe He will. Let's go guys, time is of the essence! And thanks again, Clete!"

Clete nodded and gave a wave as the group headed down the hallway. His instructions were easy enough to follow and they soon disappeared from his sight as they turned down the next hall. McCoy was a little nervous about Jim looking out of place, but his fears were soon put aside as they approached the administrative desk. Everyone there had their noses buried in their computer screens and no one even acknowledged their existence.

The next hallway was dimly lit, but the blue footprints were easy enough to follow.

"189! We're here!" Joshua called out in a hoarse whisper.

Ted peeked inside the room. It was barely lit up with a very small lamp on a stand and all he could see was a motionless figure in the bed. McCoy nodded towards the door and everyone went in. As soon as everyone was inside of the room, McCoy closed the door behind them and turned on the lights. They all paused to look at Terri Sullivan lying in the bed. Her face showed no emotion, just a blank stare. She was much like a corpse at a funeral except she was still breathing. Nothing else showed any sign there was still a life there. The silence gave the room a solemn tone. Ted was the first to speak.

"Okay, Carter, now what?"

"Well, Ted, now we figure out how to get her out of here."

"Still no plan?"

"Not yet. I'm thinking."

"I have an idea," said Joshua. All eyes in the room were on him as he spoke. "There's a gurney just up ahead in the hall. We can use that to transfer Miss Sullivan out of here. All we have to do is take her out the way we came in. The back door has a ramp we can use to easily wheel her across the parking lot."

"But won't these monitors set off an alarm? Tip them off we're taking her?" asked Ted.

"I think I have an idea for that," said Sheila. "I'm taking some of the nursing assistant classes in school. I'll put the same electrode stickers on me that she has on. There should be some stored in one of the cabinets in here. One at a time, we'll switch the wires from her to me. Without everything being disrupted at once, there's a good chance they won't notice and we can then press the reset button on the machine. I'll take her place here in the bed as a decoy till you get her back."

"And Joshua and I will stand guard so no one will get close enough to notice the difference."

"Do you see it, Ted?" asked McCoy.

"See what?"

"The Lord has brought us here together. It wasn't our plan, it was His. He put us all here together to do it. And we wouldn't have a chance unless we were all here."

"You're right on that one, Carter," replied Jim. "Joshua and Sheila both felt led to be here. They were led here so we could pull this off."

Ted couldn't argue the point because it did, in fact, seem like everything was falling into place for them. "Okay, then. We'd better get to work making this plan happen."

"I'm already one step ahead of you," said Sheila gleefully. "I've already found the electrodes and a spare gown to wear. If you gentlemen will just excuse me while I step behind this curtain and get into uniform, we'll have this part of the plan in motion."

McCoy chuckled, "Joshua, my boy, I don't know where you found this young lady friend of yours, but I recommend you keep hanging around her. She's really got her act together."

Joshua smiled at McCoy and replied, "Oh, I've seen her handle more than one crazy situation. There was this time..."

"Shush, you! Don't give up any of our secrets!" Sheila gleefully interrupted from behind the curtain. "Ready or not, here I come!" Sheila emerged from the curtain, dressed in a hospital gown with several of the electrodes showing.

"Well now," said McCoy, "I do believe you're going to be an excellent decoy!"

"I certainly hope so. You guys go get that gurney while I start switching electrodes."

"Aye, aye, captain!" Joshua playfully saluted Sheila as he and Jim left to get the gurney.

"Are you ready for this, Ted?" McCoy's voice had a very serious tone.

"We don't really have a choice at this stage, do we? What if they catch us?"

"No. There's no turning back now. And no weapon formed against us shall prosper, so success will surely be ours!"

"I wish I could be as confident as you are."

"You just have to learn how to trust, Ted. Trust in the Lord's plan for us."

Ted nodded out of politeness more than anything as Jim and Joshua returned with the gurney.

"Good timing, guys! I just finished switching the last electrode," said Sheila, smiling widely. "I did it fast enough, there was nary a beep from the monitors! We should be good to go on that front!"

"Excellent!" exclaimed McCoy. "Now let's transfer Miss Sullivan onto our gurney."

"Use those buttons there at the end to raise it up to the same level," instructed Sheila. "That will help quite a bit. And just pull the sheet she's on across evenly onto the gurney. It should be easy."

"I knew she'd come in handy," Jim said as he winked at Joshua and gave him a playful nudge with his elbow.

"How about you two become handy and get the job done?" teased Sheila.

"Yes, gentlemen, let's do this," said McCoy, "Jim, you and Joshua take that side of the sheet and pull while Ted and I lift on this side to help it slide easier."

"Okay, guys," said Ted, "we're in position. Is everybody ready?"

They all looked at Ted and nodded.

"Okay, on the count of three, Carter, you count us down."

McCoy nodded. "One. Two. THREE!"

Sullivan's body was so light, it took little effort for the four of them to transfer the body smoothly.

"Excellent! Now use the straps on the gurney to make sure she is secure!" said McCoy excitedly.

Within minutes, Sullivan was strapped securely to the gurney and Sheila took her place in the bed. Being a similar height with the same hair color, Sheila was sure to pass for Sullivan in the dimly lit room, especially if Jim and Joshua kept everyone from actually entering the room.

"It looks like we're ready to go. The Lord has provided everything here for His plan to succeed through us, thanks to Jim, Joshua, and Sheila showing up!" McCoy said, his voice obviously confident.

"We're just trying to be obedient," replied Jim. Joshua and Sheila both nodded in agreement with Jim.

"You all know what to do, then. Stall everyone so we can accomplish what we need to do until we can get Ms. Sullivan back here."

"We'll be praying for you all," said Joshua, "praying that His will be done in all this and the glory all belongs to Him."

"Thanks, young man," replied McCoy. "We'll be needing all the help we can get. Let's get going, Ted, and leave our friends to attend to business here."

Ted nodded. McCoy opened the door to the room up the whole way so Ted could push the gurney through it. Looking down at Terri Sullivan's small, seemingly lifeless body on the gurney, he couldn't help but wonder what McCoy was going to try and pull off to change it. None of it would matter unless they could get Sullivan out of there undetected, though. The nurse's station would be the first test, but it proved to be no more difficult than it was coming in. They all had their noses in their own business and paid no mind to the gurney being pushed past them by two strangers. The next obstacle would be getting her out of the building. There was no way the two of them could get the gurney out the entry door they came into without a lot of effort. It simply wasn't made to handle gurney traffic. Just as they entered the last hallway leading to the door, Clete Diehl appeared from out of a side room before them.

"This way, guys!" Clete whispered. "There's a service entrance down this way that has a ramp you can use."

"You're a lifesaver, Clete," said McCoy with a smile.

"You're too kind. Now if anyone asks, I wasn't here. Now, hurry, the security guy's due to come down this hall any minute."

"Thanks, Clete, we owe you!"

Ted pushed the gurney down the hall as McCoy went ahead.

"Here, Ted! Here's the way out!"

McCoy helped Ted navigate the gurney through the service door and down the ramp towards the van. They had the gurney successfully loaded up in no time, before anyone even knew they were there.

"Drive us back, Ted. I'm going to ride back here and start connecting the equipment to Ms. Sullivan. We'll be working through the night because we have to have her back here before the sun comes back up."

That doesn't leave us much time, Carter. Are you sure this is going to work? We'll be in super big trouble if it doesn't, you know."

"I know, Ted, I know. But we're getting to the part where the vision was very specific for me. I trust God will get us through this as He's shown me He will."

Ted jumped into the driver's seat and started up the van. "He'd better get us through this. He'd better."

17
WORKING ON TERRI SULLIVAN

It seemed like only moments passed between the time they left the nursing home and when they showed up back at McCoy's place. Only moments because Ted couldn't focus on what had just happened. It was all happening so fast, he couldn't grasp what they had just done and were about to do. Everything was a blur as they unloaded Terri Sullivan and got her down to the lab. McCoy already had a lot of the leads hooked up and ready to go before they had Sullivan in place on a special table Ted hadn't seen before. It seemed like no time at all and McCoy was ready to operate his equipment.

"Show time, eh, Carter?"

"I guess you could say that, Ted. The time is now for God to show up."

"Aren't you the one doing all the work?"

"No, Ted. God's doing the work. And He's doing it through me, by way of Bradford's body."

In all the excitement, Ted had forgotten all about Bradford. Ted took a quick glance around and found him sitting in a darkened corner on the far side of the lab, apparently asleep. At least Ted hoped he was asleep.

"Is he okay? He's very still."

"He's fine, Ted. His vital signs are displayed here on my console along with Ms. Sullivan's. That old body of mine doesn't have a lot of life left in it, but it will serve our purposes. Just in case, I have enough devices stored in my chair to keep him artificially alive long enough for you to transfer us back if necessary. He's not going to die in my body."

"Well that's a comfort...for him."

"Enough chit-chat, Ted. Would you kindly flip that switch there? The blue one on that console right there?"

"What kind of weird technology does this one fire up?"

"They call it...television. I want to catch the late news while we're working."

"You've picked a fine time to be a funny man."

Their conversation was interrupted by the voice on the TV. "...and today marked the final day of court hearings in the case of one-time famed pro-life activist, Terri Sullivan. Sullivan, who was injured during an attack on an abortion clinic seven years ago, and has been in a vegetative state ever since. After years of legal battles, the final appeal, filed by the Life Counsel in Sullivan's behalf, has been turned down. Tomorrow morning, officials from the state will be removing all life support to bring this sad tale to a conclusion...in other news..."

"Turn that thing OFF!" yelled McCoy. "As you can see, Ted, failure is not an option. The rest home will be crawling with government officials in the morning. This is very serious business."

"No pressure, Carter, no pressure." Ted hoped his lighthearted reply calmed McCoy's nerves a little.

"Sure. I hope the others are saying their prayers for us. Now, turn that computer there on."

The computer buzzed to life and the screen began to light up.

"Now hand me that vial."

Ted handed the vial McCoy pointed to over to him. McCoy immediately injected Sullivan with the purple contents of the vial. Ted could see an immediate change on the computer screen he had just turned on. He watched as an image slowly appeared on the screen. He soon realized the computer was tracking the movement of the contents of the vial through Sullivan's body.

"Is that…"

"Yes, Ted, it's tracking the movement of the serum through the bloodstream."

"I don't understand. Aren't there normal concoctions that do the same thing in modern medicine? I thought we were doing something extraordinary here."

"If it were only tracking flow through the bloodstream, yes, you'd be right. But watch what happens next."

Ted watched the screen. Before his eyes, he saw Sullivan's entire circulatory system being mapped out in red. Just when he expected it to be complete, he saw the image begin to build the outline of Sullivan's body. He was about to ask McCoy what the purpose of it was, when the images on the screen changed yet again. Now there were blue lines beginning to map themselves through the image. Then there were yellow lines. In a matter of minutes, there was a complete image of Sullivan's body, along with some sort of system mapping Ted did not understand. Ted was so engrossed by the display he was watching he hadn't noticed McCoy had switched into a surgical gown.

"Whoa! You really look like a real doctor now!"

"You forget, I am a real doctor, Ted. It's been quite awhile since I've done this sort of thing, though. Hopefully it will be like riding a bicycle."

"We didn't come this far to have you forget how to be you."

"It's about time a little spirit came out of you Ted. It's going to work. The vision showed me what I need to do. Now you need to get over there, grab a gown, and scrub up. I'll need a little help."

Ted was a little apprehensive with the thought of actually having to help McCoy. Just days before, he would have told anyone he was capable of doing anything. After spending so much time with McCoy, he felt very inadequate. McCoy's intellect combined with the faith he openly shared made him feel like he knew very little. Ted watched as McCoy turned on a few more machines. When the last machine warmed up, Ted's jaw dropped open in shock and wonder. Instead of a computer screen, the images were 3-D holographic projections. What was going on inside Sullivan's body was in front of him like a video game!

"How do you like that for diagnostic equipment, Ted?"

"Carter, I'm positively floored. How is such a thing possible?"

"This was the research I had devoted myself to for decades. This is what our friend, Ms. Wilson, so desperately wants to get her hands on. I was on the edge of so many of these breakthroughs but kept coming up empty. I was discouraged and only making halfhearted efforts...pretty close to giving up actually. And that's when I made the connection between mankind and the Creator. That changed my whole outlook on everything. That's when I started having the visions giving me all the answers to the questions I couldn't figure out on my own. The results are what you see before you."

"And you're going to operate on Sullivan based on all these images?"

"That's right, Ted. I don't have time to explain how it all works or exactly what I'm reading from this, but in a nutshell, it tells me where the impulses of her brain and spirit are in a similar manner to what you saw when Bradford and I switched bodies...only in a far more explicit and detailed manner. With this I can see where her...shall we say...circuits...are broken."

"Incredible!"

"Yes it is. Incredible beyond human understanding."

Ted watched as McCoy pushed some buttons and flipped some switches on the operating table. It slowly and smoothly flipped Sullivan over so she was positioned face down. It was then Ted could see the table was made so her head, neck, and shoulder area and left leg were exposed.

"But how did you know..." McCoy interrupted before Ted could finish his sentence.

"It was in the vision, Ted. It was in the vision. Now watch this!"

Ted thought nothing could top what he'd already seen, but he was wrong. McCoy pushed some more buttons on the console before him. Ted wasn't quite sure where they came from, but lines corresponding to the holographic projection began to appear on Sullivan's skin.

"Carter, is that what I think it is?"

"If you think those lines are guides to where to make an incision, then you'd be right."

"This is incredible!"

"It certainly is. I thought I was such a hotshot scientist with all my 'superior knowledge'...but the things the Holy Spirit revealed to me showed me just how little I actually knew. It took away my pride and showed me the importance of humility. And most importantly, it showed me how much He cared for me and how much I can accomplish if I'm obedient and let the Spirit work through me. All my years of study and research were empty...the short time spent being obedient and putting all this together under the direction of the Spirit...working with you and Bradford...has been so much more rewarding than you can ever imagine, Ted. And when this is over, I have the hope of the greatest reward possible. That of living with my Savior throughout eternity."

"Please don't talk that way Carter. I don't want to think of that."

"Think of what, Ted? My death? Pass me that scalpel, would you?"

Ted passed the scalpel to McCoy and he began to make

the incision.

"Well, yes. That."

"I'm at peace with it, Ted. You should be too. I hope when I'm gone you study every memory of what we've done together...and come to the same peace as I have. You need it. You really do."

It was all too much for Ted to comprehend. No words came to him. He simply looked back at McCoy without speaking. McCoy began to concentrate on making his incisions into the back of Sullivan's neck and upper back, pausing occasionally to check the holographic images along with the images on the monitors.

"It's working, Ted. It's working. I can see it."

"See what? What is it you see?"

"I can see the damage, Ted. I can see what I need to fix. There's some severe damage in the spinal cord area that connects her brain to her body. We can fix it!"

"But I thought that spinal stuff couldn't be fixed."

"In the natural sciences we know today...it can't. It was one of things I was researching. One of the things Wilson wanted to keep control of, take credit for all the profits in the case of a breakthrough. This is the whole reason she sent you here to babysit me, Ted."

"But if it's not possible, how are you..."

"How am I going to fix it, Ted? I was shown how to do it in my visions. My research was close, but the visions showed me the gaps I was missing, things I would have never thought of on my own, how to build this equipment from what I already had in work. And I can feel it, now, too. I can feel it."

"Feel what?"

"My hands. I can feel it in my hands. They're being guided by a higher power in this surgery. It's like they belong to someone else."

Ted laughed. "They do belong to someone else!"

McCoy chuckled. "You're right, Ted. I guess they do."

Ted moved a little closer so he could see into the

incision. Just as he did, he saw a small purple glow. McCoy saw it too.

"Do you see that, Ted? Do you see it?"

"Yes. Yes I do! What does it mean?"

"That's the short circuit in her nervous system, right there in the spinal cord. That's what we hook up again. And look, there's another break, and another."

"But how will you fix it?"

"That's what the leg is there for. Now watch closely."

Ted watched as orange flashing lines began to appear on Sullivan's leg and in the holographic image. The wonder of it all still captivated him.

"What are these lines telling you?"

"These lines are showing us healthy peripheral nerves. The ones we'll be using as patches to make a repair where things are broken."

"That sounds so simple. Why hasn't anyone else done this before?"

McCoy began making his incision in the leg as he explained. "Because this equipment pinpoints exact locations of where the work needs done. And once we harvest the donor nerve material, it needs to be run through the solution over there in those flasks to actually work."

"What's in the flasks?"

"Different concoctions of natural herbs and substances I was shown in one of my visions. It all had to be assembled and cooked very precisely."

"I hope you wrote that recipe down."

"No. I didn't."

"No? But why not? What if you forget something?"

"I was instructed in the vision not to write it down."

"But I don't understand why..."

"Ted, things like this I've found it best not to try to understand. Just accept. Accept that God knows what He's doing and have faith. If it makes you feel any better, though, I don't understand it either."

Ted didn't have a reply for McCoy's comment. He found it so unbelievable, he just stood there shaking his head in amazement. McCoy had finished harvesting the nerves necessary to make the repairs and was carrying them to the flask.

"Ted, set up the timer on that computer. These nerves must be soaked in each of the three flasks for precisely 40 seconds each. Give me the exact start and stopping point for each one."

McCoy stood poised to lower the nerves into the first flask on Ted's signal.

Ted prepared the timer. "Ready?" McCoy nodded. "Go!" The timer started immediately with the immersion of the nerves. "Stop!" McCoy raised the nerves from the flask and moved them above the second flask. "Ready?" McCoy nodded. "Go!" The nerves were dunked into the second flask. "Stop!" McCoy readied the nerves for the final flask. "Ready?" McCoy nodded. "Go!" Ted watched as McCoy calmly soaked the nerves in the final flask. "Stop!"

"Time for the moment of truth, Ted. Are you ready?"

"It's all you. Go for it!"

McCoy went back to Sullivan's body. Using a tool he specially designed for the task at hand, he carefully put the three strands of nerve where his equipment was telling him to.

"Ted, hand me that small canister from the desk. The one with the lightning bolt drawn on it."

Ted grabbed the canister and handed it to McCoy. "What's this stuff for? And is there any significance to that lightning bolt?"

"Think of it as a soldering compound as if we were joining two wires together. That's why I drew the lightning bolt on it."

"Another secret formula?"

"Yes, yes it is. This one is more like an ointment. It not only has plants in the recipe, there are also several varieties of insect included."

"Amazing."

"Yes it is. Amazing how many cures already exist in nature if we only know where to look." McCoy carefully applied the ointment to the nerves he had just repaired. "Ted, look at this!"

"What is it?"

"Look closely! The ointment is instantly bonding the nerves together! It's like all the pieces have always been a single unit! And look at our images! It's showing the flow has been restored back through these nerves! It's a success!"

"It's a miracle!" exclaimed Ted.

"Yes, it is nothing less than a miracle. All the wisdom contained in the visions worked!"

"All you have to do is stitch her back up now."

"Hand me the canister with the bolt drawn on it, please."

"You mean..."

"Yes. I was given a mixture to close the surgical incisions up too. Care to guess what's in this one?"

"Never mind. I know it's a secret, so let's just get this done."

McCoy laughed. "You're getting it, Ted, you're getting it!"

McCoy carefully applied the contents of the canister to the flesh and muscles where he had made the incisions and pressed it all together. Miraculously the wounds not only sealed up, the skin healed to the point where there was barely any evidence of an incision ever being made. Ted could tell by McCoy's expression that it had worked even better than McCoy expected.

"Do we have a spiritual crazy glue here, Carter?"

"Even better, Ted. There's not even evidence of an incision. The surgical part of this plan is complete!"

McCoy stepped back from the table and activated the switches to flip it back over so Sullivan was facing up again. It may have been his imagination, but he thought her face had a look of peace on it now.

"Are you ready Ted? Ready to see Ms. Sullivan return to the real world?"

"I can't lie, Carter. I've been tingling with amazement through this entire thing. I can hardly wait to see how this plays out."

"Hand me that hypodermic, the one right there."

Ted handed McCoy the needle. He recognized the contents to be the same as he had seen McCoy use to bring Bradford back after he had been sedated. Ted was anxious to see what Sullivan would be like after it went to work on her. Would she stay the same or come back like McCoy had said? Ted watched closely as the contents of the hypodermic slowly entered into her system. It was only moments after McCoy withdrew the needle until Ted saw it happen. He closed his eyes, rubbed them and looked again. Sure enough, Sullivan's eyes were starting to flutter. And then they opened. And then her mouth curved into a slight smile.

McCoy put his face down close to Sullivan's. "Terri? Terri? My name is Carter McCoy. Slowly concentrate on my voice. If you can hear me, blink once."

Ted's heart nearly skipped a beat when he saw Sullivan blink once.

"Terri, you've been in a coma for a very long time. Don't try to do anything too hastily. Just be calm. We have you strapped to this gurney for you own safety. We must take things slowly for your own good."

The voice was very low, very soft, and very weak, but it was heard by both of them nonetheless and there was no doubting it was coming from Sullivan's mouth. "I know."

McCoy was ecstatic. "What did I tell you, Ted? What did I tell you?"

Ted was astounded. "You've done it Carter, you've done it!"

"No, Ted. He's done it!" Carter pointed his index

finger skyward.

Sullivan's lips started moving.

"Look, Carter, she's talking again," exclaimed Ted.

McCoy put his face close to hers like before. "What is it, Terri? What is it?"

Her voice was soft and weak, but unmistakable. "I've...always...known...what was...going on...around me. Been...locked...inside."

Ted and McCoy exchanged glances. Both of them imagined the horror of being trapped in their own bodies, unable to communicate.

"Terri," McCoy spoke softly, "if you've been aware the entire time, does this mean you know of...you know of what they mean to do to you today?"

Her reply was still weak, but more forceful, "Yes!"

"Terri, listen to me carefully. The Holy Spirit gave us this plan to save you. You must trust in Him just as we have. Your body hasn't fully functioned in a very long time. Your muscle tone will take time to rebuild, but I believe you will be restored. Right now, I just want you to try to move the fingers on your hands."

The expression on Sullivan's face changed to one of determination. McCoy could tell it was taking a great effort for her to use her atrophied functions, but he could also tell she was up to the task. Slowly her fingers trembled, then wiggled and flexed.

"Terri, we have success! Your fingers are moving! Now let's try your toes."

Sullivan's face carried the same determination, but now that determination was coupled with ecstatic jubilation in knowing her fingers could once again move. Just like her fingers had, her toes began to tremble, then wiggle. This time she could tell they were moving and she laughed with happiness. A weak laugh, but a laugh nonetheless.

"More success, Terri! You'll have to go slow to build all your muscles back up, but they work!"

This time her weak voice had an unmistakable air of

happiness to it. "Thank you!"

"Don't give thanks to me, but give the glory to our Almighty God. This is all His plan. Now let me tell you about everything that will be coming up as we continue this plan."

Ted marveled at everything that had just taken place. As he watched McCoy begin to explain what Sullivan could expect to happen next, he couldn't help but notice the smile and happiness that shone from her face. Obviously the smile of a captive just released from her prison.

18
A TRIUMPHANT RETURN

"Pretty easy duty so far, eh Joshua?" Jim Dunning looked comfortable leaning on the doorpost.

"Yeah, so far. I wonder why Dr. McCoy thought it was necessary for us to guard this room?"

"Well, duh," replied Sheila in a whisper, "what do you think would happen if a comatose woman were to suddenly disappear? The whole world would be here before you could say 'kidnap' and the whole plan would be blown."

"You've got a point there, Sheila. I just wonder how the rest of the 'plan' is coming along."

"Now that you mention it, we forgot to pray for McCoy and his friend Ted," said Jim.

"Well," said Sheila, "maybe you guys should do that out in the hall. It would look pretty suspicious if someone happened to pass by here and saw a comatose woman in prayer. And give me some kind of signal if someone is coming so I can do my acting job."

"Sure thing. Just don't expect any Academy Awards for your performance," teased Joshua.

"Oh, shush, you! Get out there and get to praying!"

Jim laughed at the two of them picking on each other. "Let's get out in the hall, Joshua. Like she says, it will look a little suspicious with all this activity in the room of an alleged comatose person."

"I get ya. We'll do the heavy lifting out in the hall while sleeping beauty here gets the job of laying in bed."

"Get out of here, you buffoon!" Sheila laughed and threw a roll of surgical tape at Joshua.

Jim turned off all the lights except the small one by the bed as they were leaving. "This should be enough light for anyone to see someone's in here, but they won't realize it's not Ms. Sullivan unless they come in for a close look and find you. We'll make sure that doesn't happen."

Jim and Joshua quietly slipped out into the hallway, leaving the door to the room open just enough for someone to get a small glimpse inside.

"Prayer time," Jim said quietly. "Can you tell me anything about this Terri Sullivan so I can pray a little more specifically?"

"Terri was the first pro-life activist I ever heard of. She was pretty radical at the time, the way she fearlessly went up against the big abortion mills to protect the unborn. She made a lot of speeches and really stirred up support for the movement. I had heard rumors that what happened to her, the thing that put her in a coma, wasn't a random act of violence, but a carefully orchestrated hit to get her out of the way. Some say she was costing the abortion mills too much money."

"Sounds like a brave, courageous lady."

"She was. The bravest."

"Then we best do what we can to pull this thing off. For her sake. Time to pray."

The two of them took a spot on opposite sides of the hall and began to pray. Sometimes silent, sometimes softly spoken words, but always words of warfare for the spiritual battle they were waging. Words asking for protection and success for the plan God was putting into motion in their presence,

"Hey, you there!" The voice brought their prayer time to a halt.

"I'm sorry I interrupted your...umm...break time, but I'm looking for Terri Sullivan's room, can you please show me where it is?"

Jim wasn't sure how he felt about the woman mistaking their prayer time for sleeping on the job, but he had faith God's hand was in it. Joshua began saying a silent prayer the intruder wouldn't to anything to anger Jim.

"Who wants to know?" Jim wasn't trying to sound imposing, but his stature made it hard to not look menacing, especially in a dimly lit hallway.

"I'm Maddy Morrison, and I'm with 'The Daily Voice' newspaper. I'm doing a story about how much money it has cost the medical establishment to keep Ms. Sullivan artificially alive and how the time and resources could've been better spent in other areas. I wanted to get a head start on this story before the grand unplugging event this morning. That's when people from all over will be showing up."

"Her room is right there. But you can't go in." Jim spoke his reply softly and quietly.

"Thanks. But I have to go in. I have to get pictures to show Ms. Sullivan is not a viable human being."

"Not a viable human being?" Jim's tone got a little louder this time. Joshua hoped this woman wouldn't push him too far.

"No, sir, not a viable human being. Just like an undeveloped fetus. They offer nothing to society, so society shouldn't be expected to support them needlessly."

Jim felt his blood pressure start to rise, but he forced himself to remain calm. "How can you say what value which life has? How do you know Sullivan couldn't be eventually cured or those 'undeveloped fetuses' as you call them, have no value? You have no idea what they will contribute to society at such an early stage."

"But they are a drain and a parasite keeping a woman from reaching her potential."

"And the fetus has no potential?"

"No. It's not a person."

Jim realized a confrontation here was not in the best interests of the plan they were here to work on. "Well, miss, we'll just have to disagree on that one. I, for one, believe that little fetus is a person at the moment of conception, that all the person it is to become is already there, just waiting for the rest of the body to develop. Either way, I can't let you go in the room."

"Why not?"

Jim pointed. "See in there? She's resting peacefully, let's try not to disturb her."

"We can't disturb her, she's a vegetable!" replied Ms. Morrison with a haughty arrogance.

"I'm sorry you feel that way, ma'am, but I can't let you in."

Morrison tried to walk past Jim to go into the room, but he was prepared and did a quick sidestep to block her path.

"Let me in."

"I'm sorry, ma'am. I'm not budging." Jim was remaining calm, but Morrison was getting pushy.

"Get out of my way!"

"Sorry, ma'am." Jim wasn't budging. Morrison kept pushing, but couldn't move the big man or get past him.

"I'm going to call my boss and he's going to call yours! I'll have your job!"

Jim smiled. "I don't think you'd like my job very much, ma'am."

Joshua chuckled out loud and Maddy Morrison left, indignant, with a stream of foul language flowing through her lips as she disappeared down the hall from where she came.

"Whooped 'em again, big guy," Joshua laughed.

"Let's just hope she doesn't wake her boss. We don't need them snooping around and finding out we don't belong here."

"You're right there. I hope you bought McCoy enough time to do what he's doing."

"Amen to that, Joshua, amen to that."

Several hours passed with no further interruptions. An occasional nurse would walk by and peek in the doorway, but no one else came to enter the room. The three of them continued praying it would stay that way.

McCoy and Ted were at that moment returning to the service entrance to return a now recovering Terri Sullivan back to her room. McCoy had to keep reminding her to not wear her voice out right away. It would take some time to strengthen her voice and muscles, but she was whole again and recovering at a miraculous rate.

"We're here, Carter. How do we get back in?"

"God will provide, Ted, God will provide."

"Amen." The soft voice of Terri Sullivan still surprised the two of them.

Just then, the service door opened on its' own to reveal a smiling Clete Diehl, waving them to come in. "I thought you boys might need a little help, so I've been keeping an eye out for you. I just sent the security guy down to the cafeteria for coffee, so you have a couple minutes to sneak in here. Hurry!"

Clete rushed down the loading ramp to help Ted and McCoy push the gurney carrying Sullivan into the building. With Clete's help, it was an easy task.

"Thanks for your help again, Clete. You've been a blessing," said McCoy.

"I'm only too happy to help, sir. May God be with you!"

"He is, Clete, He is." Clete stood there stunned and unable to speak as they disappeared down the hallway. He had just been talked to by a comatose woman!

Once again, they were able to walk by the nursing

station without attracting attention. It was hard for Ms. Sullivan to keep quiet because there were so many things she wanted to tell them all as she passed by. So many years worth of things, both good and bad.

Jim and Joshua both saw Ted and McCoy approaching at the same time. After exchanging very triumphant glances, Jim nodded towards Joshua to open the door the whole way. Ted and McCoy easily made the turn to steer the gurney into the room. Jim and Joshua followed and closed the door behind them.

Jim was the first to speak. "How did it go Dr. McCoy? Was your experiment a success?"

"It most certainly was!"

Sheila bolted upright in astonishment and both Jim and Joshua's mouths dropped open as they first heard words coming from Terri Sullivan herself.

"Praise the Lord!" Joshua raised a fist skyward.

"Amen, God's done it again!" Jim joined in the praises.

"Did you bozos ever doubt He would show up?" Sheila asked, obviously happy with this new development.

"As you all can see, everything God showed me in the visions worked perfectly. Ms. Sullivan is once again back with us."

"Carter, I don't want to rain on this celebration, but we had a reporter snooping around earlier. It would probably be best if we get things back in order as quickly as possible in case someone tries to crash our party soon."

"You're right, Jim. Joshua, you and Ted help make the switch with Sheila and Terri. It shouldn't take as long this time, since Terri is able to move a little bit to help this time."

"What!? She can move too?" exclaimed Sheila.

"Yes, but not a lot just yet," replied McCoy, "her muscles are still weak, but they are functional. Apparently someone took the time to do some physical therapy for her, so she won't have to start from square one with her rehab."

"That's right," added Terri in a very quiet voice, "there was a caring nurse's aid who used to work my arms and legs for me when no one else would. She was one of the few that talked to me like I was a real person, too. People like that kept me from going completely mad. Most of them treated me like a piece of furniture. Or worse."

"You mean you knew what was going on around you?" asked Sheila with a look of shock.

"Yes. Yes I was aware of everyone around me. Every act of kindness, every act of disgust, every act of malice, every act of exploitation or ignorance. All of it. Some heart-warming, some terrifying, some sickening." Terri began to quiver a little.

"Easy Ms. Sullivan, you're safe now. You're whole. You're among friends. And most important, God is with us!" McCoy placed his hands on her to comfort her. "We'll help you deal with all of that later. Right now we need to get ready for whatever the press is going to throw at us soon. I expect them to show early, so that means we probably have little time."

The group worked as fast as they could to switch the connections from Sheila to Terri. They were all amazed how quickly she was adapting to being complete again, as if she had never been in a coma. All of them silently praised God for the miracle they were blessed to be a part of.

"Okay," said McCoy, "it looks like we've gotten Terri all hooked up to the equipment. Now let's move her into position on the bed."

Jim and Joshua gently lifted Terri from the gurney and placed her on the bed, just like she was before they took her away. The setup looked perfect!

"Mr. McCoy?" Terri's week voice was trembling.

"Yes, Terri?"

"Would you please sit here with me and hold my hand? I'm feeling some anxiety being back here in the bed after getting a taste of freedom again. This is...this is...well, it's just so hard." A tear rolled down Terri's cheek as she was speaking.

Sheila saw the tear and immediately grabbed a tissue to wipe it from her cheek. "Take care of her McCoy," Sheila said in a voice reflecting the defiance she was feeling, "the rest of us have this. We can handle any press people that show up."

McCoy smiled at Sheila as he sat down beside Terri. "I will do exactly as she wants. She's the real hero here. But there's no need for the rest of you to 'handle' the press. Just keep it from becoming a mob scene. We actually want them to come in here now that we're ready. We want them to see God's miracle. Right Terri?"

"Right, Mr. McCoy. I'm ready to leave this prison and give God all the glory."

Ted couldn't help but but feel out of place. All these people confident in their spirituality and giving God credit for everything going on around them, and here he was overwhelmed by everything. He felt helpless in the flow of the events taking place, like he was just going where the currents took him. McCoy noticed the lost look on Ted's face and had a pretty good idea what he was thinking.

"Ted, grab that chair and sit in here with Terri and me. The others can direct whatever traffic comes our way. Sit with us."

Ted pulled up the visitor's chair from the corner of the room and sat down on the other side of the hospital bed. For all the excitement going on, he couldn't help but notice the peaceful look on both McCoy and Sullivan's faces. He found himself wishing he, too, could have such peace.

"Ted, you look stressed."

Ted shook his head and raised his eyes to meet McCoy's. "How can I not be stressed? Just think of what we've done. The risks we took. And now the press will be on us soon. How are you so peaceful?"

"I'll answer that for him. It's because he knows he's

right where God wants him right now."

Ted couldn't believe Terri Sullivan was talking again. If he had gone through a fraction of what she had been through, he would be a basket case.

"She's right, Ted. God's been guiding our every step. You need to put everything aside and realize how much God loves you. There's a reason He led me to involve you in all this. I hope you find out what the reason is soon."

McCoy barely got the words out of his mouth when the sound of a huge commotion in the hallway reached their ears.

"There's the press, right on cue," said Ted, his voice betraying his agitation.

"Mr. McCoy, we need to say a quick prayer for our friends in the hall," said Terri quietly.

"You're right, Terri. You're right."

Out in the hallway, Jim, Joshua, and Sheila were being confronted by a mass of reporters and camera men. Although their arrival was expected, none of them were expecting the rude pushiness these people were displaying. None of them were displaying anything that resembled manners and the first camera man even pushed Sheila out of the way so he could be first one on the scene for his "photo op." He soon forgot about that when he found Jim blocking his path.

"Apologize to the lady."

"Move! I must capture this photo op! I can't let the moment get away!"

"I suggest you apologize to the lady before you take another step." Jim was starting to get a little bit angry at this photographer.

"Do you know who you're dealing with? Who I am?" The man was getting indignant and poked his finger into Jim's chest. He seemed to flinch a little when he discovered how solid Jim's chest was.

"Yeah, I know you. You're the guy who's going to be wearing his camera in a very unpleasant manner if he doesn't apologize to the lady like he's been asked to."

"If you don't get out of the way..."

Jim smiled and took a step forward. At the same time, a tearing sound came from the seam of the scrubs Jim was wearing. The right sleeve no longer contained Jim's bicep, something the camera man immediately noticed as his eyes widened at the sight of the now exposed muscle.

"I'll be more than happy to get out of your way. After you apologize to the lady."

"I...uh...I" It appeared to everyone there the camera man was directly addressing Jim's muscles.

"Come over here, Sheila, I think this nice man has something to say to you." Jim leaned down to look at the man directly in the eye. "You do have something to say to her, don't you?"

"Uh...uh...I'm...I'm sorry miss. I...I...should have been more considerate towards you."

"There now, that wasn't so hard was it?" Jim slapped the man on the back and nearly knocked him over. "Now with that out of the way, let me show you into the room."

"Wait!" The voice came from the rear of the group. It sounded familiar and it was. Maddy Morrison was now pushing her way past the others to reach the front.

"I was here first! A few hours ago!"

Joshua and Sheila exchanged glances, wondering what Jim would do to her. They wouldn't have to wait long to find out.

"Well, Ms. Morrison, it's good to see you again." Jim's voice sounded light and happy.

"Don't you try to sweet-talk me now. I have a letter from my boss and he has an expensive lawyer just ready to run down here."

"No need to get all excited, Ms. Morrison. I'd be happy to escort you and my new friend here right in."

Maddy Morrison was speechless for a moment. She was prepared for a big mouth battle, not getting her own way.

"You're just going to let me in?"

"Sure. Why not?"

"Well why wouldn't you let me in the last time?

"It wasn't time yet."

"And now it is?"

"Yep."

Jim stood aside and motioned for the others to follow Maddy Morrison and the camera man in, but not before he followed them in himself. There was no way he was going to let Maddy Morrison, or anyone else for that matter, get in that room without him being there to protect McCoy or Terri Sullivan. Everyone packed in the room to get a good look at the woman who the state decided would be dying today. They weren't expecting to see McCoy there holding her hand or Ted on the other side, but it didn't stop them from setting up their equipment.

"Quiet! Quiet everyone!" Morrison needed the room to be quiet for her microphone. "George...George, do you have the shot? I want Sullivan visible in the background behind me." George nodded. As soon as she was satisfied everyone was going to be quiet, Morrison began to speak into the microphone.

"Are we live?" Again, George nodded. "I'm here in the room of Terri Sullivan, former pro-life activist, who ironically will have all life support systems removed this morning and be allowed to humanely pass peacefully."

"That sounds nice, but I think I'll have to decline."

Morrison was stunned, believing she imagined the voice coming from Terri Sullivan. She turned to look and saw Terri Sullivan smiling back at her. She dropped the microphone.

"Did you get that, George?" McCoy asked, a big smile on his face. George nodded, grinning himself this time.

"Surprised, Maddy?" Terri asked quietly. "Maybe you have a few questions for me, perhaps?"

Morrison, obviously shaken, picked up her microphone.

"How…but how…just how is this possible?" Her hands were shaking as she spoke.

Terri replied quietly, "with God anything is possible, Maddy."

Morrison dropped the microphone again, sobbing heavily this time. All the reporters and cameras were working frantically to capture the scene.

McCoy turned to Terri, "why is she taking this so hard? Am I missing something here?"

Terri spoke softly so only McCoy could hear, "Maddy Morrison was one of the last people I talked to before ending up here. It was her abortion I was protesting when I was assaulted. I can't prove anything, but I think it may have been the news outfit she works for now who was behind it."

McCoy's expression immediately grew serious. "Jim, could you please clear the room for us please? And leave Ms. Morrison here."

Jim stood tall and spread his arms, now fully splitting the seams of his sleeves. "Alright everybody, you got your story. Now out of the room!"

There were a few protests, but those who were closest to Jim made no argument and convinced the others to leave without incident. George, the cameraman, made sure to keep his camera running as he walked out of the door backwards. Sheila shut the door behind him as soon as his camera lens cleared the doorway.

Jim turned around to face McCoy, "okay, doc, the room's cleared out just like you asked."

"Thanks, Jim. I think Ms. Morrison, here, needed some privacy."

Morrison was still sobbing openly. Ted got up from his chair and led her to it so she could sit down. She nodded to him in thanks, then looked at Sullivan and started sobbing even more deeply.

Terri placed her hand on Morrison. "God makes anything possible. He can restore you and give you peace."

"How can He forgive me? How can He forgive me for letting my child be aborted? How can He forgive me for...for...for what happened to you?"

"Don't limit God. He'll go to the gates of Hell to save you. His grace is more than enough to cover anything you've ever done. I can see the guilt in you you've been carrying ever since that day. Place it before the cross, before Jesus, so He can carry the burden. It's too much for you to carry alone."

"How can you be so sure?"

"All these years I was alone, alone and trapped in my body, but He was right there with me. With me so I wasn't really alone. And it's through His grace I was brought back. He gave these people the information and knowledge needed to bring me back. To bring me back...and save you."

For the first time in a long, long while, Maddy Morrison's eyes showed hope.

19
IT'S TIME

"That was quite a scene back there. Do you think Terri will get everything all worked out and back to normal?" Ted asked McCoy as they were driving back to McCoy's place.

"I have no doubt at all, Ted. No doubt at all. She seems to be so much stronger of a person than I could have ever imagined. And we left Jim, Joshua, and Sheila there to make sure she'd be okay till the proper authorities arrive. I also left information with her on how to locate her father. I'm sure a lot of people will be more than willing to provide what she needs to get back on her feet again. God put together quite a plan to bring her back."

"And for us?"

"Well, Ted, the first order of business is for me to give Bradford his body back. I'm sure he missed it."

"Well, yeah. There is that. I wish we wouldn't have to do that. I'm just really getting used to you in Bradford's body. It's been quite a ride."

"Yes it has, Ted, yes it has. But we have to do what's right. God trusted us with great things so we have to honor Him with all our decisions. Doing the right thing according to His will is how we do it."

"I suppose," sighed Ted as they pulled into McCoy's garage. The morning sun just now illuminating the entire sky.

As they entered the lab, they found Bradford sleeping in front of a television. There was a pretty good reason to believe he had watched the live feed of their exploits.

"Bradford? Bradford?" McCoy was speaking softly to try and gently waken the man sleeping in his body.

"Huh? What? What the...Oh, yeah. Hello. Sorry, for a minute there I was a bit confused. It's not every day one wakes up and looks right at their own face."

McCoy laughed. "Don't worry. It's quite understandable. It's time."

"It's time?"

"Yes. Time for you to resume residence in your own body."

Bradford laughed, "I hope you didn't wear it out. I can't lie, this hasn't been easy for me. I have a new appreciation for people whose bodies don't work the way they should now."

"I can honestly say it was miraculous to be able to know what it was like to have a young body again, too. Don't worry, I'm going to leave it as I found it. It is tempting to keep it, though." McCoy gave Bradford a wink.

"Hey!"

McCoy laughed. "Don't worry, don't worry, we're here to transfer you back right now."

Bradford got excited when he heard that. "Not a moment too soon. I'm ready! I'm ready!"

"I could take that as an insult to my body, you know," teased McCoy.

"Don't get me wrong, doc, your body was once a finely-tuned machine. It's just got way too many miles on it for my liking."

"Understood. Time to get this done. Ted, are you ready to do this again?"

"Carter, the way you've got everything set up, the equipment almost does the job by itself. It will be a breeze this time since I've done it before."

"Good. Let's get to it and start hooking Bradford up."

With the experience of doing the job before, Ted and McCoy had Bradford on the table and hooked up in no time. Of course, McCoy was able to help out with his own connections and he, too, was soon ready.

"Do it, Ted."

Ted nodded to McCoy and pushed the button to start the process. Ted wasn't sure if it was his imagination or not, but McCoy seemed to be a little anxious for some reason. Since he had done the transfer before, he knew just what to look for. The equipment did not disappoint. It was becoming so very easy and all he had to do was flip the right switch at the right time. The first time they did the transfer, it seemed like it took forever. This time, it flew by like it took no time at all. Ted pushed the last button and the transfer was done.

"Carter, are you okay? Everything work right?"

A tired voice replied, "yes, Ted. I'm back where I belong. Are you okay over there, Bradford?"

"Yahoo!! I'm me again!!"

"I'll take that as a 'yes.' Please unhook me, Ted."

"Sure thing, Carter. Glad you're okay. Bradford, you can start to...oh, never mind, I see you've already removed all your connectors."

"Sorry, Ted, my friend, I'm just too anxious to move around in my own skin again!"

"Well, move your skin over here and help me get Carter back in his chair, okay?"

"Sure thing!"

Both of them were lifting, but Ted could swear McCoy's body had gotten lighter since the last time they lifted it off the table.

"Easy now, there you go." Ted found himself instinctively being more gentle with McCoy as they lowered him into his wheelchair.

"Thanks, boys. I really feel at home now." Carter paused and looked at Ted and Bradford.

"Let's go outside now. All of us. I think I could use some air."

There weren't any words spoken as the trio rode the elevator to the garage and went outside. Ted felt the silence was awkward, but Bradford was just drinking in the freedom of being in his own body again and didn't give it any thought. McCoy led them down the sidewalk and paused in front of his house, wheeling around so he could get a good look at it all.

"I think it's time, boys. Time for me to go home."

Bradford was confused. "But you are home. This is your house right here."

"I meant my real home. My heavenly home. My eternal home with Jesus."

Ted was visibly upset. "Are you sure, Carter?"

"Ted, it says in the scriptures, if I recall correctly, in the fourth chapter of James, 'we're nothing more than a wisp of fog, catching a brief bit of sunlight before disappearing.' We're all very much like that. Just a brief time in this world to make a difference before going home to live with Jesus, our Creator. I've caught my sunlight. It's time to go."

"But what makes you so sure of this? That this Jesus cares?"

"Ted, I wasn't sure till I gave up everything to Him, let Him run things. I think it's in Psalm 103 where He tells us something like, 'He knows us inside and out...we, as humans, don't live very long; we spring up like wildflowers but like the wildflowers, pass just as quickly, leave nothing to show we were here.' But know this, Ted. It also tells us God's love is always, eternally present. When I'm gone, all I leave behind will be the memories you have Ted. I'll be gone. The love of Jesus will still be with you every step of the way for the rest of your life, Ted. Every step."

Bradford spoke softly, "I'll remember you, too, Carter. I'll never forget any of this."

"Bradford, it says in Hebrews, chapter 13, I think, to 'make sure you don't take things for granted or give up working for the common good; share what you have with others. God is particularly happy with acts of worship that take place in the workplace and streets.' Remember that, Bradford. Use your gifts for the common good of all."

Ted started to weep softly. "I'll never forget you, Carter. I'll remember all of this for as long as I live."

"Above all, remember this, Ted. It's from the first book of John. 'Wanting your own way and having everything for yourself, wanting to look like you're important to everybody, has nothing to do with Jesus. Whoever does what God wants him to do is set for eternity.' Please listen to Him, Ted. Listen to Him and have eternal life."

"This is all just so much to think about. You've tried to lead me to faith the whole time we've been together, but I'm still having trouble processing it all."

"I know, Ted. Sometimes it's extra hard with people of our scientific background, especially since a lot of the time we're trained to accept theory as fact, but if you search for truth hard enough, you'll find it. Jesus is that truth."

"Only because of you will I consider these things. If you believe it, there's something there to investigate. I know that much is true."

"Thanks for the vote of confidence, Ted, but I'm just being an obedient servant of God. We had a hand in miracles with the soul transfers we did in the lab, but the real miracle the Holy Spirit wanted in all this was to secure your soul for eternity, Ted. That's what all of this has been about from the very beginning."

"You mean..."

"Yes, Ted. This whole project...this project soul research...has always been about your soul."

"I promise I'll preserve and continue your research, Carter. It will be in your memory for as long as I live."

"No, Ted. It's not to be."

"What do you mean, 'not to be'?"

"Just what I said. All the research, all the notes, all the equipment, all of it...dies with me."

"But...everything? How can this be? You can't let it all be for nothing."

"It's not for nothing. The purpose of everything I was given in the visions has been fulfilled. It's done. In the beginning, my selfish ambition wanted my research to live on through you when I was gone, to pass it on to you. Now I know it has to end now...end with me. What I need to pass on to you, what needs to live on after me, is faith, Ted. All that's left is for me to go and for you to make a decision. I know you haven't made a decision of faith in Christ yet, but I know you won't rest until you figure it out for yourself."

"Maybe if I go over your research again..."

"No, Ted. It will be gone along with me."

"I don't understand. Is it going to magically disappear or something?"

"No. No magical disappearing act. The secrets I was given in the visions were just to bring us to this moment. If it's His will, they'll be around another time for someone else. There's a reason we're out here. I felt my body failing rapidly. The monitors are hooked up to keep track of my vital signs. When Bradford was in my body, I had it set up to revive the body and keep it alive artificially, if necessary. Now that I'm back in the body, it's set to detonate the booby traps, the explosives, and incendiary devices all over the house that I told you about before. When I go, it all goes."

"You mean…"

"Yes, Ted. I only have minutes left. The Almighty has blessed me with the wisdom to know the end is coming and to be prepared."

Ted stood there dumbfounded. Bradford had listened to their whole conversation and was envious of the bond Ted and McCoy had formed. He was also in awe of everything he had been a small part of, a witness to this incredible event. The two of them stood silently by McCoy's side, both of them now suddenly aware of a warning buzzer on the chair starting to beep.

Ted's lips quivered as he spoke, "Does that mean..."

"Yes, Ted," answered McCoy. "Remember, God loves you more than you can imagine. That goes for you too, Bradford. One more thing. I love you both."

As soon as the words left his lips, McCoy slumped over in the chair and the beeping turned to a steady alarm. Dr. Carter McCoy had gone home to be with Jesus. At the same time, sparks and small explosions started to erupt from the eaves of McCoy's house. They could hear more explosions coming from the basement laboratory. Flames were becoming visible through all with windows. Soon the entire house was engaged in flames. In his last act of thoughtfulness, McCoy had programmed lawn sprinklers to be turned on all around the house to keep the flames from going anywhere else. The two men watched in silence as the house seemingly disintegrated within minutes, two silent figures with the body of the now departed Carter McCoy between them.

20
THE DRAGON LADY DEFIED

Olivia Wilson's knuckles were turning white from how tightly she was clenching the steering wheel in her car. She was so sure she was going to get the big, executive promotion she craved. Everything was lined up for her to rise up to the top level in the corporation and it was going to be made possible from the profits she had planned on making from stealing Dr. McCoy's research. Now that plan was all but gone. When news reached her McCoy was dead and his house and everything in it had burnt to the ground, her hopes and dreams of rising to the top may as well have gone down in flames with it. Her only hope lie in Ted Crosby and how much he had learned from McCoy before he died. Just the thought of Crosby made her stomach bunch up. He wasn't as afraid of her as the others in the office were. They were easily kept under her thumb, but Crosby had that blasted streak of independence in him. It would've been a whole lot easier if she could've sent someone less intelligent to spy on McCoy, but Crosby was the only one brilliant enough to be able to relate to McCoy and actually learn from him. At least she could see that one thing working in her favor. The beat up car assigned to Crosby while he worked with McCoy was in the parking lot. Maybe he was there early because he had information and wanted to gain her favor. That thought nearly made her laugh out loud. She knew Crosby wasn't like her other employees who would do all sorts of unethical things just to please her. She'd just have to resort to the normal intimidation tactics to get him to do what she wanted. It always worked on the others, so it was sure to work on Crosby, too.

Ted was waiting patiently in Olivia Wilson's office. He was anxious to get the nasty little task of dealing with her behind him as soon as possible. Bidding his last farewells to McCoy and having to answer all the questions the authorities had for him concerning the fire really wore Ted out and left him so emotionally drained he wasn't able to sleep at all the night before. Hopefully Wilson wouldn't push him too far. He was soon to find out because he could hear the sound of her assistants kissing up to her as she approached. Oh how he loathed their phoniness! The door opened and his worst fears were realized. The grimace on her face showed she was already in a bad mood and the look of her eyes betrayed her recent use of illicit stimulants. Ted really wasn't in the mood for this kind of confrontation.

"Crosby. Good to see you're here early and ready to go."

"There's no place I'd rather be." Ted didn't try to hide the sarcasm in his voice.

"Let's get right down to it, Crosby. McCoy's dead. What did you learn from him?"

"I learned how to operate a wheelchair."

"Crosby! You know more than that! Tell me!"

Ted looked down to the floor and thought his next answer over carefully. His mind went right to McCoy and all the things they'd been through. He now knew what to do.

"I did learn something very important. I learned McCoy was the most intelligent person I've ever met. I learned his faith made him humble. And giving. And so deserving to have all the wisdom possible in this world. Something you don't qualify for."

Ted watched as Wilson's face began to turn different shades of red.

"Why you..." Wilson started into a stream of expletives, some of which Ted had never even heard before. It was obvious to him whatever her drug of choice was that day, it was starting to really kick in.

"Feel better now?"

Ted's flippant reply only sent her into a more intense rage. With no warning, he had to duck a book she threw in his direction.

"I'll make your life miserable, Crosby. No raise for you this year. Your performance record will have a black mark on it requiring your performance to be examined every three months. Three times the workload of anyone else. I'll be watching your every move closely. Very closely."

"And the alternative?"

"I don't think you want that, do you now, Crosby?" Wilson's face had a disgustingly smug sneer on it.

"Well," Ted stood up and got within inches of Wilson's face, "I've watched you harass people, make huge mistakes in the budget and fire others for it, bully the people working for you, set up a network of snitches and reward them for ratting on people...no, Ms. Wilson, I think what I don't want is to be around unethical and immoral people like you. I chose the alternative." Ted began walking toward the door.

"Crosby, if you walk out that door, there's no turning back!"

Ted whirled around to face her once more. "And just what makes you think I'd want to come back? The fact of the matter is, Ms. Wilson, that I began to lose interest in working here quite some time ago. You might think working here is a special privilege, but I know better now. I knew someone like you only looks out for yourself and doesn't care about the people under you unless you can use them to better your own status. McCoy knew that, too. He was always a step ahead of your treachery. You don't deserve to walk the same planet he did, let alone profit from his ideas. As long as I live, you will never get anything, not a single shred of information on McCoy's work, from me. Ever!"

Ted turned and walked out the door, never looking back. Olivia Wilson just stood there shocked as he left. Ted meant every word he said to her, but knew in her drugged-up condition, it was possible she wouldn't remember for sure if any of what had just happened was real or not. He was sure, though, all the words from McCoy he remembered were real. It was during the exchange with Wilson the truth behind McCoy's words shot right through his heart. He needed to talk to someone. He needed someone to explain things to him. He needed to talk to Pastor Carson as soon as he could.

21
PROJECT SOUL EXPLAINED

When Ted left the company parking lot, he headed straight out of town and over the mountain towards Pastor Max Carson's church. There was plenty of daylight left, so he got to enjoy the scenery along the way. As he climbed higher, he could see a number of farm fields, all decked out in differing shades of green, depending upon what was growing in them. A few fields had cattle grazing in them. Ted suddenly realized he was enjoying the beauty of it all, something he would have never done before his time with McCoy. Their little bit of time together had changed him and he hadn't even realized it. He should've known, though. If it weren't for McCoy, he wouldn't have the questions for Pastor Carson he needed answers to. If it weren't for McCoy, he wouldn't even know of Pastor Carson or Carson's friends, Jim, Joshua, and Sheila. And Clete. How could he forget about Clete Diehl? Those people all seemed like one family instead of individuals. Come to think of it, he and McCoy had formed a similar bond. Maybe this spiritual thing McCoy always talked about was the common denominator. Ted was really hoping Carson would have time to talk to him. That made him laugh out loud. He was in such a hurry to make this trip he had never bothered contacting Pastor Carson to see if he could talk. But there was just something inside telling him to go. Normally that would've made him feel a little weird, but after hanging around McCoy who spent his last days talking about little else but how he was being led by his visions and that mysterious "Holy Spirit" of his, it seemed so normal. He hoped Pastor Carson was ready to do a lot of explaining. All the thoughts bouncing around in Ted's head caused him to lose track of time. Before he knew it, he was there, pulling in to the parking lot of the Brooksville Community Church. There was another car in the parking lot, one that looked very familiar. Ted dismissed the familiarity as a coincidence, though. There was no way it could belong to who he thought it did. Ted looked at it closely as he parked beside it. Just no way. It wasn't even a possibility. Instead of continuing with that thought, Ted began noticing the flowers along the sidewalk. The last time he was there, it was too dark to notice there were even flowers there. Now he was drinking in all the colors and savoring the aroma of the blossoms. He was so entranced by the flowers when he looked up and saw someone was standing in the door waiting for him he nearly jumped a foot out of surprise.

"Welcome, stranger! It's about time you got here!" Jim had a big smile on his face. Joshua and Sheila peeked out from behind him and were smiling too.

Ted felt confused. "Were you...were you all here waiting for me?"

"Sure was. Come on in. Make yourself at home."

Ted felt stunned. Even more so when he walked inside and found Bradford was there too. It *was* his car outside!

"Well, Ted, long time, no see," said Bradford, smiling.

"I wasn't expecting to see you here."

"I wasn't expecting to be here. But there was something stronger than me pulling me in this direction.

Something I didn't understand. Then I remembered McCoy talking about finding answers here, so I knew this was the place to be."

"Yeah, me too."

"We were waiting here for you, Ted. Bradford was just a bonus," said Pastor Carson.

"What!?" Ted wasn't sure if he was hearing things right.

"This whole thing, Ted. Carter felt it early on. He told me everything. His visions were in a large part about saving Terri Sullivan, but from the very beginning, he told me it was about saving you, Ted. He called it 'Project Soul,' because he wanted to save your soul. In you, he saw himself as a young man. He wanted to keep you from wasting so much of your life pursuing science without knowing Jesus, the Creator, the One behind everything scientific. He wanted you to live the life he wished he could've lived."

Ted knelt down and began crying. It was just as McCoy had told him before. All the thoughts, all the memories, what Pastor Carson was saying, was all coming together for him. He was beginning to understand how deeply McCoy had cared for him and even more important, how much the Jesus McCoy believed in cared for him too. The others sensed it was the beginning of a new life for Ted and gathered around him praying. Bradford sat in amazement and took the whole scene playing out before him in.

Pastor Carson knelt beside Ted, speaking softly, "Ted, Carter McCoy did a lot of amazing things for mankind in the name of science. Things that will be what he will probably be remembered by, perhaps forever. But the greatest thing...the single most important thing he did...something he probably won't get any credit for...well, that thing is being obedient to our Lord, something he didn't learn about till later in life. It was that obedience that showed him how to bring Terri Sullivan back to life, back to a life that will potentially save an untold number of unborn children. Only God can know how much of an impact that obedience, the obedience of one man, will have on the world. And God would know this because of the obedience of another single man, His son, Jesus. The One who took on all the sins of mankind so we could live with Him eternally. All of us, Ted. Including you."

Ted turned to Pastor Carson, "I can see that now. Carter told me about this and I didn't see it then. But I do now. I believe. I do believe. I believe Jesus died for me. I believe He is the Son of God and came back from the dead. Came back for me. And sent Carter to help me see the truth."

"That's right, Ted. Because you believe that and confess it as truth, you'll get to see Carter again. We all will."

"Pastor Carson, I don't know if this is a good time to bring this up or not, but it's something that's been bothering me the whole way over here. I'm not quite sure what to make of it and I thought maybe you could help me figure it out. I barely slept at all last night, but when I did, I had a dream. In the dream, Carter was there with me. We got in his van, and I was driving out through the countryside. We went past some old houses in a small town and he pointed out one in particular. He didn't say anything, but somehow I knew immediately this particular house was the one he was born in. We continued driving, and went past many different houses and towns, and again I somehow knew each different place represented a different part of his life. He seemed to have a sadness about his face, like he was going to miss his old life. It wasn't an intense sadness, but almost like he was going to miss the people and places he was leaving behind. We went a little further through some very beautiful countryside and soon came to a gate. Carter looked at me with his sad face, and then gave me a big smile as if to tell me everything was alright. We both got out and approached the gate. A group of people, all happy and smiling, came over to greet Carter and welcome him. They only smiled and nodded to me. One of them opened the gate for Carter and he went inside, never once looking back at me. It was then that I noticed he was walking up a path that led to a magnificent palace. As I was looking at the palace, all the people that came to greet him began to tell me what a wonderful place it was, the most magnificent place that could ever be. In the distance I saw Carter enter a door in the front of the palace. All the people stopped talking to me, yet continued to smile at me warmly. I turned and got back in the van. As soon as the van door closed, I woke up."

"Ted, I believe you've had your first vision. The Holy Spirit allowed you to go along with Carter as he entered the gates of Heaven."

"Really?"

"Yes, most visions have a lot of symbolic images and scenes and that's how I would interpret yours. If you keep having them, and keep seeking wisdom from the Holy Spirit, you'll understand them much better."

"Wow. So this is the kind of thing Carter was doing all the time?"

"Carter was really in touch with his visions. So much more than anyone I've ever known. I guess that's why he was given the wisdom to do the things he did. It was something no one but him was capable of. God's perfect plan."

Bradford spoke up, "It was a perfect plan, Ted. Carter wanted to save your soul and not only did he do that...well, he saved me too. Our brother, Jim, led me to the Lord before Pastor Carson showed up. It was all because of the stuff McCoy kept telling us at the lab. It all makes sense now. Because of McCoy's faith, we're all in the family of God now. Along with our friends here, we'll be hanging around with McCoy again someday."

"That's it!" exclaimed Ted, "that's how we're a family! We're all brothers and sisters in God's family!"

"That's right, Ted. We're all family now," said Pastor Carson. "McCoy's Project Soul was a success and brought you, and Bradford, into the family. Now it's time for the rest of us to take McCoy's Project Soul even further and bring others to faith in Christ so they can be in God's family, too."

"I'm not sure how I'll fit into this," said Bradford, "but the first thing I'm going to do is use some of my financial resources to get the Sullivans back on their feet. And to fund some of my new brother Ted's work. I think there's some amazing things ahead of him."

"There's one thing I'm sure of," said Joshua, "Project Soul is for all of us to work on. It's just the beginning."

"Amen to that, Joshua," said Sheila, "Amen to that."

Ephesians (The Message Bible) -3:20 God can do anything, you know—far more than you could ever imagine or guess or request in your wildest dreams! He does it not by pushing us around but by working within us, his Spirit deeply and gently within us.

ABOUT THE AUTHOR

The author was born, raised, and has spent his entire life living in Pennsylvania where each day contains the magnificent marvels of God's grace and wonders of His creation all around. The primary goal of this story is to strengthen faith and bring new souls into eternity. This is the true "Project Soul" of this story.

If you like this story, tell your friends. Please read the other novels by D.L. Ford. You'll be glad you did! (And so will I!) Visit *www.dlfordbooks.com* for more information on these stories!

"The Jesus Rock"
"The Trials of Jim Dunning"
"The Mysterious Tunnel"

41251157R00116

Made in the USA
Middletown, DE
05 April 2019